Trapped in a cave with no one to help them . . .

Molly stared at the water trickling into the cave. With the next wave, she knew, the trickle would become a torrent. Each wave would raise the water level bit by bit. "We have to make a break for it, Ashley," she said. "If we wait much longer, we won't be able to get out at all."

Ashley began to quiver from head to foot. "I can't. I can't face it. It was hard enough to crawl through before. I just can't do it again with sea water washing over me."

Molly jumped away from the dark tunnel entrance as another wave washed through it, spilling onto the floor in a foaming swirl.

Ashley looked at her, pale and wide-eyed. "This is it," she said in a small voice. "We're stuck."

"No," Molly said with new resolve. "If we don't do something, we'll die." Molly wasn't about to accept defeat. She realized she had to be strong for herself and for Ashley. She had to think of something. But what?

An Angel
for Molly

FOREVER ANGELS

An Angel
for Molly

Suzanne Weyn

Troll

Published by Troll Communications L.L.C.

Printed in the United States of America.

10   9   8   7   6   5   4   3   2   1

For my parents, Ted and Jacqueline Weyn,
who first gave me the words and pictures
which are my tools.
—SW

1

People said Molly Morgan was pretty. Some people even said she was beautiful.

They were wrong.

"I just don't see it," Molly said, glancing into the mirror above her white dresser. What she *did* see was a thirteen-year-old girl with waist-length, white-blonde hair, sea-green eyes, and a clear bone-china complexion. She was also very thin, but that was another thing Molly couldn't really see.

She was trying to see it, though. "You're thin enough. You're thin enough. You're thin enough," she chanted to her mirrored image over and over until it sounded like Yurthinny Nuf.

When Molly was in the hospital a few months back, she'd laughed to herself, imagining a glamorous, pleasantly plump movie star named Yurthinny Nuf. During her therapy sessions, whenever Dr. Harding told Molly, "You're thin enough," Molly imagined the diamond-decked Ms. Nuf standing behind him eating a fat, gooey piece of chocolate cake.

It made Molly laugh. It also helped with her therapy. If Yurthinny could eat so much and still be so stunning, Molly could, too. Right?

Then Molly wouldn't have to starve herself.

She wouldn't have to die of anorexia.

A knock on her bedroom door broke her reverie. Molly opened it to find Joy, their housekeeper, standing outside.

"Morning, Molly," Joy greeted her cheerfully. "Your father wanted me to tell you he'd like to talk to you before you leave for school. He's in the morning room."

"All right," Molly said. "Do you know what it's about?"

"No, but he's in a good mood about *something* this morning." Joy winked broadly at Molly.

"Okay. Thanks." Molly couldn't help smiling. Joy's usual happy disposition was catching. "I'll be down in ten minutes."

Molly shut her door as Joy turned to leave. Her father was in a good mood? Well, at least that meant *she* hadn't done something wrong. What could he be so upbeat about? He wasn't exactly Mr. Merry. Sometimes she even referred to him behind his back as Commander Demander because he was so stern and strict.

Molly turned from the mirror and opened her closet door. Stylish new shoes sat in a row, neatly lined up on the gleaming wood floor. She picked up the square-toed black Mary Janes with the fat brass buckle, her current favorites. They'd go well with today's outfit, a short, flared black dress with soft gray tights. Then Molly reached in and grabbed a vest with dazzling gold-thread embroidery against a black background. It was perfect, just the right finishing touch.

As she sat on the edge of her canopied bed buckling her shoes, Molly thought about anorexia. What a weird disease. Even though the scale had said she was only eighty-five pounds when she went into the hospital, she'd been so sure the scale was wrong. She'd been so sure she *was* fat. All she'd had to do was look in the mirror. It seemed so obvious.

But her eyes had been playing tricks on her. Molly understood that now. Her mind had tricked her. It was still a daily struggle, but she was on her way to recovering. Every week she talked to Dr. Harding and felt a little better about things.

But it wasn't only the therapy that had made the big difference. It wasn't only gaining enough weight to get out of the hospital, either. Not really.

It was the angel.

Her meeting with the angel had given her the strength to recover. More than any other single thing, Molly could thank the angel she was still alive.

Lately, though, the warm feelings of love and acceptance the angel had given her seemed to be fading. Without an angel there to help her every day, it was getting harder and harder to hold onto the good feeling of being lovable just the way she was.

"Molly!" Her mother's smooth, aristocratic voice floated down the hall outside her closed door. "Molly, dear, you don't want to be late for school."

"I'm coming," Molly called. She slid off her bed. Impulsively, on her way out, she stopped to open her top drawer. She took a glossy brochure from among her neatly arranged socks and tights. Looking down at the rocket on its cover, she sighed longingly. How wonderful it must be, traveling in space. Folding the brochure carefully in half, Molly slid it into her dress pocket and stepped out into the long white-carpeted hallway.

Today would be a good day to show it to her mother. A distant, white winter sun blazed warmly through the tall windows at either end of the hall. Molly had gotten enough sleep. She was in a good mood and felt brave. Today she felt up to the challenge of countering all the arguments.

Downstairs, she found her mother in the morning room, a glassed-in breakfast nook facing out onto the garden. Molly glanced out quickly. The formal, square hedges were finally losing the last of their leaves. The fountain was empty, drained for the winter.

Delicate-featured Mrs. Morgan sat in the shiny, deep green leather booth, drinking coffee and reading the society column in the newspaper. She turned the page with one impeccably manicured finger before looking up and noticing Molly. "Good morning, dear," she said, gracefully inclining her sleek blonde head. "You look lovely today, Molly. What a clever combination."

"Uh, thanks," Molly said, heartened by the compliment. This was a good sign. Today *was* a good day to approach her parents. Molly looked around for her father. "Joy said Dad wanted to see me."

"Yes, I do," her father said as he came into the breakfast area. He was a tall man with dark hair just beginning to turn gray at the temples. His height and booming voice with its slight British accent made it seem as if he completely filled the room when he entered. He always seemed to be the center of everyone's attention no matter where he was. Today he was magnificently dressed, as usual, in one of the incredibly expensive suits he had specially made by London's world-famous Savile Row tailors whenever he was there on business.

Molly studied him, trying to tell if he seemed excited, in a good mood about something. Yes, there was a sparkle in his deep blue eyes that transformed his usually steady gaze. "I've just made a new investment," he said proudly.

No news there. Molly's father was always making investments that Molly understood nothing about. Mrs. Morgan rolled her eyes before turning back to the newspaper.

"What kind of investment?" Molly asked.

"A racehorse," Mr. Morgan said. "An Irish champion."

"For real?" Molly cried. "That is so cool!"

"Ian, I really can't believe you've gone and done this. *What* are you going to do with a racehorse? I mean, really!" Mrs. Morgan said in a dry, droll voice.

"Race him, of course. This horse is a sound investment, Cynthia. Extremely sound."

"What is wrong with investing in stocks and bonds?" Mrs. Morgan asked. "A racehorse is so . . . so high-maintenance."

Mr. Morgan sighed. "I was fortunate to learn that Lucky Feather was going up for auction. It was sheer chance, really. Buying him is just the same as buying a promising stock."

"Lucky Feather," Molly repeated. "Nice name."

Mr. Morgan nodded. "Yes, indeed. Excuse me a moment while I get my tea." He seemed deep in thought as he headed into the kitchen.

"Have some breakfast, dear," Mrs. Morgan told Molly. The words, *I'm not hungry*, leapt to Molly's lips but she fought them. She knew she *should* eat. She reached into the basket on the table and took out a warm buttered bagel. "Good girl," her mother said approvingly as Molly bit into the bagel.

Mr. Morgan returned carrying a cup of tea and sat beside Molly and across from his wife.

"Did you want to ask me something?" Molly asked him.

"Yes. I did," her father said, taking a sip from his steaming mug. "I wanted to talk to you about those new friends of yours. Don't they work on a horse ranch or own it or something?"

"You mean Ashley and Christina," Molly answered. "Ashley's parents own the ranch and Christina's mother works there. She and Christina live at the ranch, too."

"And the other one, what's her name again?" Mrs. Morgan asked.

"Katie," Molly replied. "But she doesn't live on the ranch. She's just friends with us."

"Oh, that's right," Mrs. Morgan said.

Molly knew her mother didn't really like her new friends. She didn't understand why Molly was no longer hanging out with the kids she used to be friends with—the kids who came from Pine Ridge Estates, the wealthy neighborhood where the Morgans lived.

Molly couldn't go back to hanging out with those kids. Not in a million years. She almost wished she could, though, just to please her parents. She knew she'd upset them enough with her anorexia. She hated to give them anything else to worry about.

But she couldn't bear it. Now, after all she'd been through, it was easy to see how shallow and self-centered most of her old, so-called friends really were. Molly had even begun to suspect that the only reason they'd liked her in the first place was because her parents had so much money. When she was in the hospital, Ashley, Katie, and Christina had all sent cards and come to visit. None of her other friends, except her sort-of-boyfriend Matt, had so much as called.

No, Molly couldn't go back and act as if nothing had happened. But she knew that her change of friends was one more thing to puzzle and disturb her parents.

Dr. Harding said she should be less concerned about upsetting them. She was *too* good. Molly didn't understand that. Weren't you supposed to be good? She'd always done all she could to please her mother and father. It was just how she was.

Molly couldn't tell her parents how she felt. Despite all their family counseling, Molly still had a hard time talking to them about her real feelings. How could she tell them that she felt nothing she did was good enough for them? It would just upset them. *And* they'd deny it, so what would be the point? She especially couldn't tell them about the angel. Then they'd think she was really crazy. She'd *never* be done with therapy if she told them about the angel.

"Anyway, about your friends," Mr. Morgan said, bringing the conversation back to its starting point. "I'm asking about them because I need a crew of horse handlers to help me fly Lucky Feather back from Ireland and I was thinking they might be good people to get in touch with."

Molly's jaw dropped. This *was* exciting. "Sure. Sure. They could do it. Ashley and Christina have been around horses all their lives."

"I'd need more than two girls," Mr. Morgan said. "I'll call the ranch and speak to the parents. Do you have the number?"

"Sure, I have it right here." Molly rummaged in her backpack, her mind racing wildly. It seemed as if her father was serious about this. He was actually going to take her friends—and their parents, of course—to Ireland to get this incredible racehorse. A new thought struck her. Why couldn't Molly go, too? He was her own father, after all. Why couldn't he take her, too?

There. She found her cellular phone in the bottom of the bag and pulled it out. Struggling to remain calm, she carefully pressed a button. Ashley's number lit up on the tiny screen.

"Here it is, Dad," Molly said, handing him the phone. Her fingers shook a little from excitement, but her father didn't seem to notice. Good. Molly knew she had to be careful how she asked her question. If her parents thought she was *too* excited about going, they might worry about how it could affect her health. Then they'd never agree.

"Dad?" Molly began.

"Yes, Molly?" he said, looking up from his pocket diary where he'd copied down the phone number. He fixed his direct gaze on Molly and she felt her courage waver.

Better just blurt it out and get it over with, she thought. "Dad, please, can I go with you? To get Lucky Feather?"

Mr. Morgan's eyes widened in surprise. Molly had never asked to go on a business trip with him before.

Surely he could see that this was different. Her friends would be going. It was a trip to bring back a racehorse. "Please," she said again.

"School," Mrs. Morgan reminded her.

"We have Thanksgiving vacation next week," Molly said beseechingly, her eyes darting back and forth between her parents. "We have a whole week and a half off, sort of a fall vacation. That would be a perfect time to go."

"I don't know," Mr. Morgan said. "This is a serious business trip, not playtime. I won't be able to spend a lot of time sightseeing or anything like that."

"That's all right. And you know I'm good around horses," Molly said. "You know that. Haven't I taken *dressage* lessons at the club for years?"

"Let me think about it," Mr. Morgan said, setting down his mug with a thunk of finality. He stood and kissed Mrs. Morgan on the cheek. "I'm off," he said with a quick smile. "Have a good day, Molly."

"You, too," Molly replied, trying to keep the sullenness she felt out of her voice. Why couldn't he have just said, "Great! Come along with me, Molly. We'll have so much fun." No, instead he had to *think* about it. That *really* made her feel wanted.

Molly watched him walk out of the kitchen.

"It's just that he's not used to having you along on a business trip," Mrs. Morgan said gently, correctly reading Molly's expression. "I think you took him by surprise."

"But this isn't a regular business trip," Molly argued. "He's getting a horse!"

"I know. Really, your father. I don't know what's gotten into him," Mrs. Morgan sighed. "Buying a racehorse."

"Why does he have to think about it? Why can't he just say yes?" Molly asked angrily. Did he dislike spending time with her so much? "Are you going?"

"Oh, no. I can't," Mrs. Morgan said. "Ireland is beautiful this time of year, but I have to work on the fund-raiser for the hospital. I wish I could go, especially if you end up going, too, Molly," she said wistfully.

She picked up an envelope she had tucked under her placemat. "By the way, dear. This came yesterday and you need to fill it out fairly soon."

Glancing at the clock to see how much time she had before school, Molly absently took the envelope from her mother. She read the return address on the envelope. "Camp Silver Lake? What do they want in November?"

"They want to get you pre-registered again this year. It's a good idea, so you can select your cabin before the desirable ones get filled up." Molly's mother nodded knowingly. "You remember how unhappy you were the year you got stuck in the cabin next to the woods."

Molly had spent every summer since she was six years old at Camp Silver Lake . The place was all right. She had some friends who went there, and they did interesting things. They had been interesting the first few times she'd done them, anyway. But by last year they'd started to seem old and boring.

This year Molly had something else in mind. She slid the glossy pamphlet from her dress pocket and handed it to her mother. "It's funny that the Silver Lake stuff came, because I was just about to show you this," she said carefully.

Mrs. Morgan's eyes goggled at the words written across the pamphlet in bold red, white, and blue letters. "Molly, dear, you can't be serious!" she said, leaning back against the booth.

"I am serious," Molly said firmly. "That's what I want to do this summer."

"But, sweetheart, your . . . *condition*."

Molly stood up angrily. "I don't have a *condition* anymore, Mother. I'm one hundred and twelve pounds. That's a normal weight. I'm eating now. See!" Desperately, she ripped out a chunk of bagel and stuffed it in her mouth.

"All right, I get your point," Mrs. Morgan said. "But, Molly, are you sure going to Space Camp is what you really want to do?"

"Mom, it's just a week. I'll go to Camp Silver Lake afterwards," Molly said. "And yes, I want to do this—more than anything I've ever wanted before."

"Since when do you want to be an astronaut?" her mother asked, surprised.

"I want to find out if it's right for me." Molly held her ground. "I don't think it's an unreasonable thing to ask," she added bravely.

Mrs. Morgan winced. "But, but being an astronaut is for girls who are . . . are . . ."

"Smart?" Molly offered.

"Academically inclined," Mrs. Morgan rephrased it tactfully. "I know you're smart, but there's a lot of school involved in becoming an astronaut, and I had the idea school wasn't one of your favorite things."

"I could get my grades up," Molly insisted. She knew she didn't give school her best effort. If she did—if she had a reason to—she knew she could do it. "I will, if you'll let me go. Please, Mom, it's just a week. What could a week at Space Camp hurt?"

"Why don't you take it easy this summer," Mrs. Morgan suggested gently. "After all you've been through, you might not need any new challenges just now. You need to get back on track."

"I am on track," Molly insisted.

"Please, Molly," Mrs. Morgan said. "Dr. Harding said you don't need pressure right now. Space Camp sounds so rigorous. I would just worry about you too much."

Molly nodded sadly but compliantly. She hadn't really given up, she just didn't want to fight with her mother. She hated fighting with her. She wanted to live in a nice, happy family where everyone got along and cared about one another. If Molly didn't make trouble, that's what she'd have. She'd already caused her parents enough trouble with her anorexia. The way she looked at it, she owed them some peace.

Mrs. Morgan sighed. "Dr. Harding *did* also say we should try to be more aware of what *you* want to do." She considered. "What if I speak to your father about taking you to Ireland with him? That might help. Would that make you happy?" she asked hopefully.

"Yes, I'd like that a lot," Molly said honestly. "Would you, Mom, would you really?"

"On the condition that you forget Space Camp for now," her mother said calmly.

Molly felt cornered. This wasn't fair. But if she didn't agree, then maybe she wouldn't get to go to Space Camp *or* to Ireland. "All right," she said, resigned.

Her mother smiled. "Sweetheart, I'm so happy to hear that. I'll speak to your father today."

2

"Ireland!" Christina cried as she and Molly were swept along in the steady stream of students on their way to the cafeteria. "Ireland. How completely cool! Totally awesome," Christina continued, tossing her long, yellow hair over one shoulder as they walked.

Molly smiled. One thing Christina had was lots of enthusiasm. When she was behind something, she was behind it one thousand percent. It was such a great change from Molly's old friends from Pine Ridge Estates who were so *cool* and amused about everything. Way too cool to ever act excited about anything.

Christina was too busy embracing the universe, wanting to understand everything about it, to be that kind of affected cool. She wasn't like anyone else Molly had ever met. She didn't even *look* like anyone else. Molly thought she was completely gorgeous with her tall, willowy body and broad shoulders, her mass of flowing hair and her huge, incredibly blue eyes. Even the small white scar across her left eyebrow was interesting.

Today Christina wore a tie-dyed jumper of many swirling colors. It cheered Molly just to look at it. Becoming friends with Christina was one of the best things that had happened to her since she got out of the hospital.

"It *is* cool," Molly agreed. "But I had to make a trade in order to go. I had to give up my chance to go to Space Camp."

"Space Camp?" Christina raised her eyebrows.

"I want to go to Space Camp at the Kennedy Space Center in Florida," Molly explained. "For one week, you live like an astronaut. You even get to go on a simulated space mission. You don't have to go to Space Camp to be an astronaut, but it would give me a really good idea if that's what I want to do, you know, as a career."

"Is that what you're thinking about?" Christina asked. "I didn't know that."

"I've been thinking about it a lot," Molly admitted.

"My mother doesn't want me to go, though. She says she's worried about my health. That's what she says, anyway," Molly added bitterly.

"What do you mean?" Christina looked puzzled.

Molly sighed. "I think my mom just doesn't think I have what it takes to be an astronaut."

"She didn't say that, though," Christina pointed out.

"She didn't have to," Molly said. "I could tell that's what she was thinking."

"Are you sure?" Christina said. "It seems to me you're reading an awful lot into it. You *were* pretty sick, you know."

"Pretty sure," Molly replied. "My parents have this idea about me. They think I'm just one big problem. You know, somebody who can't really do anything right. *Especially* since I got sick."

"Why would they think that?" Christina asked reasonably. "You're popular in school. And you're not failing your courses or anything, and you don't get in trouble."

Molly shrugged. "I don't know. I just get the feeling they always expect me to do better than I do. They want me to be great all the time. And I'm just average. When I bring home a B on a test my father says, 'Not bad. Next time it will be an A.' When I get second in dressage, my mom says, 'Next time you'll be first. Sometimes I get the feeling they wish they had a different daughter, someone who always got straight A's, someone who had a million trophies and awards."

"Maybe you're wrong," Christina said gently. "Anyway what made you want to become an astronaut?"

"Welllll," Molly stalled, wondering if she should tell Christina the truth. It wasn't that she didn't trust her. It was just that the truth was . . . well . . . strange.

Christina waited expectantly, her blue eyes bright and deep as a sunny sky. There was something in Christina's eyes that made Molly feel she could say anything to her. "I dreamed it," Molly confided.

Christina's mouth opened but she didn't speak.

"It's crazy, isn't it?" Molly said, suddenly feeling foolish.

"*Crazy*?" Christina said, aghast. "Dreams are *not* crazy. Dreams are . . ." She waved her arms as if searching the air for the right word. "Dreams are our wings!"

Molly grasped Christina's strong, lanky arm. "I can't believe you just said that."

"What?" Christina faced her, excited.

"Wings!" Molly exclaimed. "I can't believe you used the word 'wings' because my dream was about angels."

"Angels," Christina gasped, her voice a whisper. "You dreamed of angels?" She linked her arm through Molly's and guided her through the steadily moving students off to a corner. "Tell me about the dream," she said excitedly. "It could be very important. Dreaming of angels is always very significant."

"I don't know about that. I don't usually put much importance in dreams," Molly began self-consciously.

Christina tugged at her sleeve. "Just tell me, quick."

"All right. It was a simple dream. I dreamed I was floating in outer space. The stars and planets were all around me. My arms were outstretched and there was an angel on either side of me. Each angel touched my elbows with only one finger on each hand but it was enough to keep me from being frightened."

"*That* is an important dream," Christina said.

"What do you think it means?"

"I'm not sure. But it seems very meaningful. Angels in outer space. That's *got* to be deep. What do *you* think it means?"

"I don't know, either," Molly told her. "But I had the dream two weeks ago and since then all I can think about is space." She gazed into Christina's clear eyes. "Christina, I want to get into space so badly now. I imagine the stars burning all around me. And it seems so vast and amazing. So limitless. It's practically all I think about."

Christina nodded. "It's your destiny. Your mother will

just have to change her mind. One person should never stand in the way of another person's destiny."

"My destiny," Molly murmured. It sounded so momentous put that way.

"Did you talk to your father about it yet?" Christina wanted to know.

Molly shook her head. "My father doesn't usually deal with stuff like that."

"Like what?"

"Family stuff. My mother makes all those decisions," Molly told her.

"Wow," Christina said sadly. "That sounds like my family."

Molly hesitated. "But . . . but . . . your father doesn't live with you."

"That's what I mean," Christina said. "I don't even know him at all. He left when I was a baby."

Molly thought about this for a moment. Sometimes it did feel like that at her house. Her father was there. She could see him. But it was as if he wasn't there, too. He was usually too busy to do things with Molly and her mother. He didn't make any decisions that really affected them.

They continued toward the cafeteria, each girl deep in thought. Molly had never before thought of herself as even *having* a destiny. What was destiny? It was fate. But what was that?

"Do you believe in fate and destiny?" she asked Christina as they went through the double doors leading into the crowded, noisy cafeteria.

Without hesitation, Christina nodded. "Sure. How

could there be fortune-telling without fate?"

Molly had never thought of it that way. "I'm not sure I believe in fortune-telling," she admitted.

"All right then, how could there be psychic intuition without fate?"

Molly knew where Christina was coming from on that one. Christina had great hunches. She definitely seemed touched with some ability that enabled her to know small, odd things. "I don't know," Molly admitted.

"I think it has to do with time," Christina began, obviously warming to the subject. "I think time exists in many different dimensions, sort of like the same movie showing on a lot of screens at once. But every screen is showing a different part of the movie. So, you could look at one screen and see the beginning of the movie, or switch to another and see the middle."

As Molly and Christina talked, they reached a table in the middle of the cafeteria where two girls sat, already eating lunch.

Ashley was petite and pretty with an exuberant mane of glowing red curls and a wash of light freckles across her face. She wore a crisp white shirt with a western-style bolo tie. Her jeans, as usual, were neatly pressed.

Katie, on the other side of the table, was tall and slim with high cheekbones, a full mouth and intense amber brown eyes. Her shoulder-length brown hair was pulled back in a ponytail. Today she wore a baseball cap with the brim turned to the back. The sleeves of her washed-out blue sweatshirt were casually pulled up to her elbows as she leaned on the table.

"Hi, guys," Molly said as she pulled out a chair beside Katie.

"Hi," Ashley greeted her. "Does this look too awful?" she asked, holding out a delicate hand with perfectly shaped and polished pink nails.

"Does what look awful?" Molly wondered. "Your hand looks fine."

"Good," Ashley said with a satisfied smile. "My nail chipped and I had a slightly different color nail polish in my pack. I fixed it with that, but then I thought it might look weird."

"I never met anyone who was more concerned about their nails," Katie said, laughing. Her joking smile faded as she scrutinized Molly and Christina intently."You guys look serious. What's up?" she asked.

"We were discussing fate," Christina informed her.

Katie slumped in her chair and threw back her head despairingly. "Oh, give me a break! Please!"

Molly smiled to herself. Katie had *no* patience with this kind of conversation. She was logical, hard-headed, and wanted just the facts. At least that was how she presented herself.

"Fate, huh?" Ashley said, sitting forward, her green eyes bright with interest. "Christina, did you tell her your idea about the movie screens?"

"No! Not the movie screen theory again. That's the craziest thing I've ever heard!" Katie cried. "Don't get her started. Let's just have one conversation that's not completely weird. Can't we change the subject?"

"I'm not changing the subject, but I have to go buy lunch," Christina said. "Are you coming, Molly?"

"No, thanks," Molly said. A stern look from Christina made her reach into her small leather shoulder bag for her change purse. "Here," she said, handing Christina three quarters. "Would you get me one of those big soft pretzels?"

"That's not really enough, but all right," Christina grumbled, heading up toward the lunch line.

Molly leaned over the table. "I have pretty cool news." She told Ashley and Katie all about Lucky Feather and the trip to Ireland.

"Do you really think he'd let us go and help with the horse?" Ashley asked eagerly. "I'd do it for free. He wouldn't have to pay me anything."

"It's probably up to your parents if you get to go or not," Molly said. "He wants to hire you to do it. He's calling the ranch today. You should warn them, though. He can be a huge pain in the neck."

"Commander Demander, I remember you telling me," Ashley said.

Christina returned with her tray and handed Molly her pretzel. "I told them about Ireland," Molly told her.

"Isn't it great? A trip to Ireland," Christina sighed. "I wonder if we'll really get to go."

Ashley closed her green eyes and crossed her fingers on both hands. "I hope, I hope, I hope," she repeated like a prayer.

Katie dragged her fork through her mashed potatoes, making a four-pronged line across them. Molly could see she felt bad about being left out of any possibility of going along. Molly wished she could say something, but what was there to say?

*   *   *

After school, Matt Larson stopped by Molly's locker. He was a tall, good-looking boy with long brown hair and wire rim glasses. He and Molly had been kind of a couple for almost a year now.

Molly shut her locker and smiled up at him as she shrugged into her red wool jacket. "Hi, Matt."

"Well?" he asked. "Was today the big day? Did you work up the nerve to ask about Space Camp?"

"Mom shot me right out of the sky," Molly reported.

"Bummer," Matt sympathized, shoving his hands into his jeans pockets. "Any chance she'll change her mind?"

Molly sighed miserably as they walked down the hall together. "Uh-uh. But I got her to agree to let me go to Ireland with my father if I don't ask about Space Camp anymore."

Matt stared at her for a moment. "Ireland?" he asked.

Molly explained to him about Lucky Feather and the trip. "I want to go to Ireland, but I want to go to Space Camp, too," she concluded.

"Ireland is cool. But lately you've been talking about space so much. I mean, I thought it was super important to you. Why did you give up so easily?"

"I was afraid I wouldn't get to do either one if I didn't compromise."

"Maybe," Matt said reluctantly. "Still, it seems like you caved in pretty easily."

"You don't think I'm crazy to want to be an astronaut, do you?" Molly asked him.

"No way," Matt said with certainty. "What's crazy about being an astronaut? I mean, it's the future."

That was one of the things Molly liked most about

Matt. He thought everything was possible. When she'd told him about seeing the angel, he'd believed her right away. "Why not?" he'd said. "Anything is possible."

"What about your father?" Matt wanted to know. "Did you ask *him*?"

"I can't talk to him," Molly said. "The minute I start talking he gets this bored look on his face. Either bored or distracted, like he's pretending to listen but he's really thinking about the stock market or something."

Matt frowned thoughtfully. "Still . . . it's worth a try, isn't it?"

"I guess so, but it won't be easy. He doesn't really listen," Molly said helplessly.

"Just get him to agree. Who cares if he really listens?"

Molly cared. She wanted him to *see* her, to care about who she was. She wished he would be proud of her. But he was so distant—there, in her house, but not really there at all.

*   *   *

When Molly got home from school, she went directly to her father's study and knocked on the door. "Come in," he called.

Stepping inside the cool, shadowy office with its paneled walls and tall bookshelves, Molly felt as if she were entering a secret place. Her father sat behind his large desk in a black leather chair, staring intently at his computer.

Molly came up beside him and peered at the screen. Colored bars and numbers filled it. He entered a line of new numbers on the screen, then looked up at Molly. At that moment, his black cordless phone rang. "Ian Morgan," he answered tersely.

With a sigh, Molly plunked into the high-backed chair beside the desk while he spoke to someone about how many shares of a stock to sell. It was always like this. Someone was always on the other end of the phone wanting his attention regarding money. Molly was used to waiting.

While he talked, Molly couldn't help looking at the papers on his desk. She leaned forward in her chair as she realized they were several different sketches of a horse.

Molly picked up the papers, four in all. Each quick, efficient pencil sketch showed the horse from a different angle. On the last sketch, a picture of a castle had been added in the background.

Molly studied the sketches. They were good, obviously done by a trained artist. "Who did these?" Molly asked curiously when her father hung up.

Brusquely, Mr. Morgan reached for the drawings. "No one," he told her. "No one you know. They're just some sketches of Lucky Feather." He opened a desk drawer and carelessly tossed the sketches inside.

"What's the castle?" Molly persisted.

"My castle," Mr. Morgan said briefly, looking back at his monitor.

"What?" Molly gasped. "*Your castle?*"

Mr. Morgan nodded. "It's been in our family for ages. I haven't been there in years, but that's where we'll be staying when we go to get Lucky Feather. It's big enough to house the whole crew. Much better than putting everyone up in a hotel."

Molly was so astounded she could no longer remain seated. She stood and walked in a small circle before she could find words. "You mean we own a castle and you never told me?"

Mr. Morgan shrugged, typing something into his computer. "I forget it even exists most of the time. But I'm glad it came up. I have to write to the grounds-keeper who lives in Kylemore and have him open up the place."

A castle. *A castle!* "Dad, you have to let me come with you. You have to!" Molly pleaded shamelessly.

"Yes, Molly. Your mother and I spoke earlier, and she convinced me it would be good therapy for you to travel. You can come, but this is business. I won't have time for sightseeing or anything like that," he reminded her.

"That's okay," Molly said excitedly. "Did you call the ranch?"

"Yes." He pushed his chair back. "In fact, I can't really talk because I'm heading over there right now."

"Can I come?"

Again, he looked surprised by her interest. "It will probably be boring. We're just going over details, flight arrangements and things like that."

Just once Molly wished he'd say, "Sure, come on." That he'd show in some little way that he would enjoy spending time with her, that he liked her.

But there was no use expecting miracles. She did want a ride to the ranch, however. She wanted to tell her friends she was going to Ireland for sure, and to find out if they'd be able to go, as well.

"Please take me. I like going to the ranch," Molly pressed. It was true.

Mr. Morgan studied Molly a moment. "All right, come along if you'd like."

"Thanks," Molly said. "Don't worry. I won't bother you at all."

3

"This is it," Molly said, and Mr. Morgan turned his silver BMW sports car into the dirt road of Pine Manor Ranch. To the left they could see horses grazing on the rolling pastures of straw-colored winter grass. Miles of neat white fences outlined the paddocks and pastures of the sprawling horse ranch.

As they drove, Molly gazed out the window to her right, staring into the Pine Manor woods thick with deep green pines whispering together in the chill breeze. It was in those ancient, mysterious woods that she'd encountered the angel on the Angels Crossing Bridge.

Molly looked over at her father and studied his handsome profile, his strong chin, his straight nose. They'd barely spoken the whole way over. Surely they could find *something* to talk about. Dr. Harding had advised her to try to be truthful with her parents, to share her real feelings and concerns. It wasn't easy, but she may as well start somewhere. "Dad?" she began.

"Mmmm?" he answered distractedly as he gazed out the window at the horses.

"Do you think I'd make a good astronaut?"

"Absolutely," he said. Molly could tell from his voice that he wasn't even listening. As usual.

"Did you even hear me?" she asked sternly.

Mr. Morgan snapped to attention. "Sorry, no, I guess I was looking at the horses. What did you say?"

"Do you think I'd make a good astronaut?" she repeated.

"Is that what you want to be?" he asked with incredulous laughter.

"Yes," Molly said stiffly. Why did he have to doubt her? Why did he have to laugh?

"Is that the latest craze?" he wondered aloud.

"No, it's what *I'd* like to do," she said, annoyed at his attitude.

He laughed again and shook his head. "I don't think you realize how much school it takes to become an astronaut. It's not easy, you know."

"You don't think I could do it?" Molly asked, hurt. "Is that it?"

"It's not that but . . . well . . . somehow I can't see it," her father confessed.

"What *do* you see me doing?" she demanded.

"Oh, Molly, I don't know," he said impatiently. "I see you being just like your mother when you grow up, running social events for charity, being active at the club. Why all these questions all of a sudden? What happened to 'I won't bother you'?"

Molly just shook her head wordlessly. She blinked

back hot tears and gulped, praying he wouldn't notice her distress. What was the use of talking to him? Why did she even imagine it was possible? He had no idea who she was. None. Worse, he didn't care.

Mr. Morgan parked the car in front of a neat, pale yellow ranch house. A golden retriever wandered lazily over from the porch and sniffed the car curiously. Ashley came out the front door along with a kind-faced woman with short red hair.

"Hi, I'm Judy Kingsley," Ashley's mother introduced herself. "I hear you have a champion who needs moving."

Mr. Morgan shook her hand cordially. "And I need a crew to move him."

"Well, you've come to the right place," Ashley said pleasantly. "My parents are the best and, naturally, I've been working on the ranch all my life. You might say horses are in my blood. Christina, too. Horses just love us. And we love them."

Molly looked at the ground, smiling to herself at Ashley's shameless sales pitch. When Ashley went after something, she could be pretty dauntless. That trait often got her into trouble at school, though her good-natured charm usually got her out again.

Mr. Morgan smiled indulgently at Ashley, then turned to Mrs. Kingsley. "Is your husband home? I'd like to discuss the financial arrangements."

"He's out on a trail ride, but I take care of the finances here at the ranch. Why don't you come inside and have a lemonade while we discuss matters," Mrs. Kingsley said.

"Very good," Mr. Morgan agreed. He followed Mrs. Kingsley up the porch steps.

Molly looked down the dirt road and saw Christina and Katie approaching on horseback. Katie rode a chestnut brown horse and Christina sat atop a palomino. Christina rode naturally, as if she were part of the horse. Katie, a beginner, sat uneasily on her mount.

"Are you guys coming in or going out?" Ashley asked Christina and Katie when they joined the group.

"Christina just gave me a riding lesson," Katie said. "But we thought we'd take a trail ride in the woods. Want to come?"

Ashley looked at Molly. "Come on. Let's take a ride."

Molly followed Ashley into the stable. She picked a horse named Clover and saddled up. Even though she'd taken riding lessons at the club for seven years, she still wasn't as at home around horses as Ashley. But then Ashley had grown up with horses.

"Ready?" Ashley asked as she led her own horse from its stall.

"Almost," Molly replied, tightening the girth beneath Clover's belly.

Ashley, Katie, and Christina were waiting outside when Molly walked her horse out of the stable. "Let's go," Ashley said. They rode into the thick pine forest, following the winding dirt trail. The wind in the pines made the needles rub against one another. The sound made Molly think of forest fairies sighing in the trees.

"The bridge?" Christina asked. The girls looked at one another. They knew she meant the Angels Crossing Bridge.

"What for?" Katie asked.

"No reason," Christina said. "Just to go. I want to look at it."

"All right," Ashley agreed, gently clicking to her horse. "Let's go."

Molly's heartbeat quickened as she followed the others off the path. She hadn't been back to the bridge since that day, the day she'd seen the angel. The thought of going back made her a little nervous. Would she meet another angel? What would happen if she did?

They rode in silence for awhile. The further they went, the darker and more still the woods became. The air became clearer, and cooler, almost icy. Molly felt she was entering a timeless place apart from the rest of the world.

"Do you think your parents will let you go?" Molly asked as they rode. She didn't have to explain where.

"Mom said she didn't know. They'll have to talk to your father before they decide," Ashley replied. "Probably, though. She said if I don't have school, then probably."

"My mother says if she goes, I can go, even if she has to pay for it herself," Christina told them.

"Guess what," Molly said. "We'll be staying in a real castle."

"A castle!" Ashley cried, astounded. "A castle. Imagine."

"That's what *I'll* be doing. Imagining," Katie said bitterly.

The girls looked at one another uneasily. The idea of leaving Katie behind made all of them more than a little uncomfortable.

"Maybe if you paid your plane fare you could stay with us though," Ashley suggested, looking at Molly for confirmation.

"That would probably be all right," Molly agreed. She couldn't imagine why it wouldn't be.

Katie laughed. "Oh, yeah, I just happen to have plane fare in my piggy bank." Katie's parents had died not that long ago in a car accident. Since then she'd lived with her aunt and uncle who had to struggle to make financial ends meet.

The friends continued riding in silence until they came to a hill. When they reached the top they looked down on an old-fashioned covered bridge that spanned a glistening creek. The canopy of pine branches split to let in sunlight that lit up the roof of the bridge and sparkled on the moving water.

Molly let all the sounds wash over her—the murmuring pines, the singing water, the varied calls of the different birds. There was another sound, though. Something she couldn't identify.

"Someone's playing music," Christina observed.

"It's just the water," Katie said, looking around.

"No, listen," Christina insisted.

Molly strained to hear. Music. Definitely. Like the tinkling of bells, the notes of a flute danced along the breeze.

"It's coming from the other side of the bridge," Ashley said as she headed her horse down the slope.

Molly and the others followed Ashley as she entered the bridge. The horses' clacking footfalls echoed on the wooden floor.

At the other side, they turned to the left and walked the horses carefully along the rocky slope leading down to the creek.

Suddenly, Clover stopped short and reared slightly. Molly picked herself up higher in the saddle to look through his pricked up ears.

Her jaw dropped at the sight in front of her.

In the chilled, rushing water of the creek, a breathtakingly beautiful woman sat in a ladder-back chair playing the flute. Her thick, blonde hair fell around her like golden waves. She wore a shimmering silver gown, clasped at one shoulder with a blue-green stone. The bottom of her gown floated, dancing on the rushing water which coursed around her ankles.

The classical music was lively and bright. She closed her eyes as she played, seemingly unaware of the four young riders on horseback who stood at the water's edge staring at her, wide-eyed.

Molly walked Clover up alongside Christina. "Is that . . . is that an . . . . No, it isn't. Is it? I mean, just because we're near the bridge doesn't mean she has to be. But she looks familiar. I've seen her before. Is she an . . .?"

"Yes," Christina said. "She's an angel."

"We're still not one hundred percent sure about that," Katie added from the other side of Christina.

"Oh, come on, don't tell me you're *still* not convinced!" Christina gasped.

"I believe in angels," Katie admitted grudgingly. "I'm just not sure that these three kooks are angels."

"What three kooks?" Molly asked.

"The woman playing the flute is Edwina," Ashley

explained. "I don't know where Ned and Norma are. They live here in the woods. And *I* believe they are angels, but we've never been able to absolutely, positively, one hundred percent prove that they are."

"Friends!" came a laughter-filled voice to their right. The girls turned sharply and saw a tall man with shoulder-length blond hair wearing a loose, white poet's shirt with full sleeves above brown leggings. He stood atop a large boulder.

Beside him on the boulder stood a dignified young woman with long jet-black hair, dressed in a silky green dress.

Molly looked hard at them. They seemed to have appeared out of nowhere.

Ned leapt lightly from the boulder into the water, Norma right behind him. They linked arms and began dancing, kicking up shimmering silver sprays of water as they turned first one way, then the other. "Join us," Ned invited the girls.

"Aren't they cold?" Molly asked as a gust of late autumn breeze swept past them.

"I guess not," Ashley answered.

The girls looked at each other. *Should* they get down and join the dancers? It seemed so ridiculous. And cold! Yet . . . there was something in the music and uninhibited gaiety of the dancers that was contagious. Molly found herself moving in her saddle, her feet bouncing in their stirrups.

Christina swung her leg across her saddle and climbed down. Without a word, she walked to the creek's edge and pulled off her riding boots and socks.

"You're crazy," Katie told her.

Christina dipped a bare toe into the creek. "It's warm." She sloshed through the water over to where Ned and Norma danced. Ned reached out and took Christina's hand, raising it high in the air. Smiling radiantly, Christina danced along with Ned and Norma.

Ashley was the next to dismount. Taking off her boots, she, too, joined the dancers.

"Oh, why not?" Katie said, grinning recklessly as she slid off her horse.

Molly sat on top of Clover and watched. Hand in hand, the girls danced with Ned and Norma, laughing and happy. Molly longed to get off her horse and join them, but for some reason she didn't understand, she couldn't bring herself to do it.

Was she afraid? And, if so, of what? Of the cold creek? Of seeming foolish? Of Ned and Norma?

Yes. Yes, she was afraid of all those things. Yet, she didn't understand why. Why couldn't she just get down and go?

She remained on Clover and watched her friends dance with the angels. Was *this* her fate—to stand by, frozen with fear as life went on around her? She hated to think that was true. It was too awful a fate. She sat forward, longing to join in the eccentric but utterly joyful dance.

But she couldn't. She simply couldn't do it.

4

At sunset, Molly's father drove down the dirt drive leading to Katie's house. The tall house was slightly dilapidated and its roof sagged a little on one side. Across from the house, a rust-red barn leaned tiredly toward the road.

Molly glanced at her father's serious, unreadable expression as he surveyed the place. Molly wished the house had a fresh coat of paint, something to make it look nicer. She wanted her father to approve of her new friends. No one in Pine Ridge Estates ever let their home get this shabby.

"Thanks for the ride home," Katie said as she climbed out. "Can you stay for a while?"

Molly looked at her father. "Can I?"

"I suppose so," Mr. Morgan agreed slowly. "But not for long. I'm going to the club for a little while. Then I'll swing back and pick you up on the way home."

"Thanks," Molly said, sliding out of the car.

Molly and Katie watched him drive away. "Well, your

dad sure didn't seem impressed when he saw this place," Katie said lightly.

"I don't think he even thought about it," Molly lied guiltily.

"That's okay," Katie said with a shrug.

"It's not that bad," Molly said politely. "It's got a lot of . . . charm."

Katie just rolled her eyes. "You get used to it. Come on inside."

Molly followed Katie into an airy country kitchen. She nearly tripped over the large, black dog flopped down near the doorway. "Move, Dizzy," Katie ordered the dog as she gently nudged him out of the way with her foot.

"Is that you, honey?" a pleasant sing-song voice chimed from another room. A short, plump woman appeared in the doorway. A halo of tightly permed, glowing blonde hair framed her rosy, smiling face. Her stout form was swathed in a neon-pink muu muu.

"Hi, Aunt Rainie," Katie said. "This is my friend, Molly."

"Hi, Molly, pleased to meet you." She looked over at Katie. "How was everything at the ranch?"

"Molly's father is taking everyone to a castle in Ireland," Katie reported as she yanked open the refrigerator.

"Don't ruin your appetite, sweetie. It'll be dinnertime soon," Aunt Rainie said. "What do you mean, a castle in Ireland?"

"It's a family castle," Molly explained.

Sharing the story between them, Molly and Katie explained to Aunt Rainie about Lucky Feather and the trip to go get him. "Mr. Morgan worked the whole thing out with the Kingsleys," Katie concluded. "It's all set."

Aunt Rainie clapped her hands together excitedly. "Katie, you're going to Ireland. What an opportunity!"

"Oh, no. I'm not going," Katie clarified, her eyes studying the worn linoleum as intently as if some fascinating movie were playing on it.

"You're not?"

"No. I'm still new to horses. I sure can't handle them like an expert. Mr. Morgan doesn't need *me*."

Molly saw an opportunity and boldly seized it. "If Katie could get a plane ticket, I'm sure there would be room for her at the castle. It *is* a castle, after all. It must be pretty huge."

Katie glared at her. Molly reddened, realizing she'd done something embarrassing.

"Forget it, Aunt Rainie. I know we can't afford it," Katie told her aunt. "It's okay."

"Would you like to go if you could, honey?" Aunt Rainie asked softly.

Molly felt terrible. The look in the woman's eyes was so filled with unhappiness.

"Yeah. Who wouldn't? I suppose I'm a little bummed about missing out," Katie admitted honestly, then she shrugged. "That's the breaks, I guess."

"I'm sorry," Aunt Rainie said.

"No sweat," Katie told her, casually pulling her thick brown hair from its scrunchy and causing it to bounce around her broad shoulders. "Is it all right if Molly and I go up to my room?"

"Of course," Aunt Rainie said absently, deep in thought.

"Go right ahead. We'll eat when your uncle and Mel come home. Molly, would you like to stay for supper?"

"No, but thank you," Molly answered politely. "My father is coming to pick me up in a little while."

Molly followed Katie into the shadowy living room. "Good move," Katie said with a smile. "You *don't* want to know about Aunt Rainie's cooking. It's the pits."

"That's not why I'm not staying. My father really is coming back soon," Molly said self-consciously. "You heard him."

They climbed the narrow stairs to Katie's room on the second floor. "Cool wallpaper," Molly commented, striding to the middle of the room and taking in the metallic silver wallpaper with black line drawings of cherubs all over it.

"You *like* this?" Katie asked incredulously, wrinkling her nose.

"Yeah. It's . . . like . . . so bad, it's good, if you know what I mean."

"I guess," Katie laughed. "That's one way of looking at it. I always thought it was so ugly it was horrible. I'll try thinking of it as cool instead."

Katie threw herself lightly onto her twin bed. With an unhappy *mrreowwww* a tiger-striped kitten sprang to its feet. "Sorry to wreck your catnap, Nagle," she said, lifting him up. His scrawny legs danced in the air, but a warm purr hummed from him like a motor.

"He's cute," Molly said, scratching him between the ears. "Where'd the name come from?"

"It's an anagram for angel," Katie explained.

"Anagram?" Molly questioned.

"Yeah. You know. A word made with the same letters as another word. Like 'dear' is an anagram for read. Same letters."

"I get it," Molly said. "Angel, Nagle. Same letters."

"Once, when I really needed help, I met someone named Nagle. He was a cab driver," Katie explained.

"Was he really an angel?" Molly asked.

Katie nodded. "I think so."

"What about today?" Molly said, sitting on the end of Molly's bed. "You don't think Edwina, Ned, and Norma are?"

"I don't know if they are or not," Katie said, frowning thoughtfully. "I like them a lot. They are pretty amazing. Sometimes I'm *sure* they're angels. Then, other times, I think they're just three loopy weirdoes who live in the woods."

"You do believe in angels, don't you?" Molly pressed.

Katie considered one of the shiny cherubs on the wall for a moment, then sighed. "Do we have to talk about this?" she asked finally.

"I wouldn't ask if I didn't really want to know," Molly told her truthfully.

"Well, yes," Katie admitted. "I mean, I have to, don't I? I've seen them with my own eyes. We all have. You know that. You saw them, too."

Molly nodded. "I know. It's just so *hard* to believe, especially after time passes. You start to doubt it. I do, anyway."

"Me, too," Katie said, scratching Nagle's belly as he gleefully kicked his legs in the air. "I know exactly what you mean."

"How do you find your angel again when you need help?" Molly asked.

"Do you need help?" Katie asked, looking directly at Molly.

"No," Molly answered quickly, uncertain if this was the honest answer. She didn't need help, not exactly. Yet she had an uneasy feeling lately. Something inside her felt nervous, restless. She found it hard to sit still. Was she slipping back? she wondered anxiously. Was the anorexia hovering somewhere nearby, waiting to ambush her when she wasn't thinking about it? In a way, she thought it was, though she had no idea why.

"I was only wondering," Molly added.

"I'm not exactly sure how you find them again," Katie replied, wrinkling her brow thoughtfully. "You could try going back to the bridge. Sometimes it just helps to ask."

"Ask who?"

"Your angel, I guess. You say, 'I sure could use some help.'"

Molly stretched across the end of the bed, propping her head on her bent arm. "That's all?" she asked.

"I suppose. I mean, I've asked for help but I'm not sure exactly what words I used. I was just sort of asking the air for help. But it was like the angels heard me. Sometimes I haven't even asked out loud."

Molly suddenly had an idea. "Could you ask for a plane ticket?"

Katie considered this a moment as she continued scratching Nagle, then she shook her head. "I don't think you should ask for stuff like that. Somehow it seems to me you shouldn't ask for help unless you *really* need it."

"You really need a plane ticket."

"Nah," Katie told her. "I'd really *like* a plane ticket." She wriggled her house keys from her front jeans pocket and dangled them over Nagle's head. The kitten jumped at them playfully.

"I wish you could go," Molly said passionately. "I mean, it's so awful and unfair that you can't." In Molly's entire life, she'd never been stopped from doing anything because of money. She couldn't really imagine how it felt. In fact, until now, she'd never even *tried* to imagine it. She hadn't even known anyone who had to worry about money. She wished she had money of her own to offer Katie.

"When my parents were alive there was more money. Not a ton of money, but more," Katie said. "Maybe I could have gone if . . ." Katie tossed the keys onto the bed and turned her face away.

Molly felt as if she should say something comforting, but she couldn't find any words. She sat up and stretched one hand toward her friend. Katie turned back abruptly and Molly yanked her hand away self-consciously.

Katie didn't seem to notice. Her eyes had taken on a hard, set look. "Anyway, Aunt Rainie and Uncle Jeff don't have money to spare, so that's that." Her face softened again as she rolled Nagle around on the bed. "Too bad, though. I'd love to go. It would be great to write a story about living in a castle. It would make a good horror story. No, a fantasy adventure. Maybe both. I don't get something, though. I thought your father was English. How come he has a castle in Ireland?"

"I don't know," Molly said. "I know we have Irish

relatives." Molly felt funny admitting this. Why didn't she know more about her father's family? she wondered. She knew about her mother's side. The family had made their money from fabric mills, and they'd been wealthy and lived in America since forever. She often saw her grandparents on her mother's side.

But her father rarely spoke of his family. She'd met her English grandfather only once when she was five. All she remembered was that he was tall and unsmiling. She'd found him frightening.

"Sorry to seem nosy. A writer needs to get into those kinds of details," Katie said knowingly.

"You want to be a writer?" Molly asked. "I mean, a real writer?"

"Yep. I'm going to be."

Molly already knew Katie wrote for the school paper, *The Writer*, but she hadn't realized she was so serious about it.

"I've been thinking of becoming an astronaut," Molly told her.

"Cool! Very cool! You know, astronaut means star traveler," Katie said, gathering Nagle in the crook of her arm. "I just read that yesterday." Katie scrutinized Molly, her amber brown eyes narrowed. "I can't believe you want to be an astronaut."

"Why not?" Molly asked, folding her arms.

"It just doesn't seem like you," Katie said bluntly.

"How do I seem?"

Katie cocked her head as she thought about this question. "Well, at first I thought you were the biggest snob on the planet," she stated.

Inside, Molly cringed. "Why?" she asked carefully.

"Because you hung out with all the snotty kids who wouldn't even say hello to you if you weren't rich," Katie said. "They probably aren't all that bad. But they aren't all that friendly, either. Admit it, if you don't have the right clothes or you aren't a cheerleader or whatever, you don't rate with them."

"That's true," Molly conceded. "But I didn't see that then."

"I know, because you were like that then," Katie said.

Molly's eyes went wide with surprise. She wasn't truly shocked at the content of Katie's words. Deep down, she knew they were true. She was simply amazed by Katie's bold, tactless honesty. That's how Katie was, though.

"But you've changed a lot," Katie added, probably in response to Molly's aghast expression. "You're nicer and more interesting than I thought. What did you like about those kids anyway? I don't get it."

Molly had to give that some thought. She'd never sat down and analyzed it. It had just happened.

"They were the kids I grew up with," she began. "We all went to Little Pine Nursery School together. They all live at Pine Ridge Estates. A lot of them go to Camp Silver Lake in the summer. I was . . . used to them, I guess."

"What made you change your mind about them?" Katie asked.

Molly laughed, feeling a little cornered by all these questions. "Are you interviewing me for the school paper or something?" she joked.

Katie blushed slightly. "No, I'm just curious. You see,

before my parents died, I went to school with a lot of rich girls."

"You did?" Molly asked, surprised. She could never imagine Katie in any other life but here in Pine Ridge. Yet she knew from Christina that things had been totally different for Katie before her parents' car accident.

"We weren't rich or anything," Katie said. "But my mother was an English teacher at this really fancy school, so I got to go for free. You and your friends reminded me of a lot of the girls there. Some of them were nice, but even the nice ones confused me. I didn't really understand why they did some of the things they did."

"Like what kinds of things?" Molly asked.

Katie shrugged, thinking. "Like, one girl, who I always thought was cool, ran away from home because she got caught cheating on a test. She was gone for days, and when they found her she was so upset and depressed, they had to take her out of school and send her somewhere for treatment."

"What didn't you understand about that?" Molly asked. She understood it perfectly.

"For one thing, cheating is something I don't understand. But the other, main, thing is that I don't see why she had to run away from home over it. So she got caught. It wasn't like they were going to put her in jail because of it."

"Pressure," Molly said as an explanation.

"What?"

Molly got off the bed and walked to Katie's window. Somehow she always preferred to walk when she was thinking hard about something. It helped her find the words, and this was hard for her to put into words. "Pressure," she repeated slowly, staring at the last of the sunset glowing pink and gold through the swaying pines. "A lot of my friends feel it. Their parents have big jobs and earn barrels of money. They expect their kids to do the same—which is probably why that girl felt she had to cheat in the first place. When she got caught, she felt like she'd blown it, like her parents would never forgive her—for failing, or even needing to cheat."

"That's dumb," Katie scoffed.

"It might seem dumb to you, but it's not dumb when that's how you feel," Molly insisted.

"Yeah, I suppose. So what made you change your mind about your friends?" Katie asked again.

"The hospital, I think," Molly answered, still staring out the window. The pink and gold sky was quickly turning a deep purple. "Of all my old friends, no one but Matt came to see me. You, Ashley, and Christina came, though. It meant a lot to me."

"Of course we came," Katie said. "You were in the hospital."

"That's how *you* are. My old friends acted like what I had was contagious, like if they even called me—which they didn't—they'd catch it."

"You must have felt terrible. I'm sorry that happened to you," Katie said.

Molly turned back to her. "Don't be. I learned a lot. I'm stronger, and I ditched a bunch of friends who weren't really friends." Sure, it had hurt then, but it didn't hurt anymore.

Nagle had fallen asleep in a ball and Katie gently pushed him to a corner of the bed. "Why do you . . ." She stopped and laughed softly. "This is the last question, I promise. Why do you want to be an astronaut?"

Before Molly could answer, there was a knock at the door. "Come in," Katie called.

Aunt Rainie stepped into the room. "I'm sorry to interrupt, but I have something important to talk to you about, Katie," she said, "and it just can't wait."

Molly stood. "I can go downstairs and wait for my father," she offered tactfully.

"Stay, why don't you?" Aunt Rainie said as she plumped down on the bed beside Katie. "Katie, I want to buy you that plane ticket so you can go to Ireland with your friends."

Katie's jaw dropped. "What? But how? I don't get it."

Aunt Rainie's soft smile was tinged with sadness. "Your parents had life insurance and other money that's yours now. We've been holding it aside for college and your future after that. But I think your parents would want you to use some of it for this trip. After all, travel is one of the most educational things you can do. And a chance like this doesn't come along that often."

Katie's eyes were wide. Her mouth was open, but she was speechless.

"That's great!" Molly cried.

Aunt Rainie gazed steadily at Katie. "What do you think, honey? Aren't you happy now?"

Katie threw her arms around her aunt and buried her head in her shoulder. When she looked up, her eyes were wet with tears she quickly brushed away. "Thank you," she said in a husky voice. "Thank you so much, Aunt Rainie."

Aunt Rainie squeezed her tight. Tears sprang into her eyes as well. "You're welcome, sweetie. Your mom and dad would want you to have this." Molly buried her head in her aunt's shoulder once more.

Molly looked on, happy for Katie. Now she'd get to go after all. What a nice woman her aunt was. Maybe they didn't have a lot of money, but they sure had what counted. Katie was lucky to live here with them.

Molly smiled as she watched Katie continue to hug her aunt. Aunt Rainie kept a tight hold on her niece. But the corners of Molly's smile drooped slightly when her mind wandered and she thought about her own life.

When was the last time her parents had hugged her like that? She thought about it a moment before realizing there was no last time.

They never had hugged her like that, not in her entire life.

5

Molly and Christina peered across the aisle of the plane to where Ashley sat, pale and gripping the arms of her seat with white-knuckled hands. She'd never flown before, and had suddenly discovered, just before boarding, that it terrified her. They'd actually had to take her arms and help her aboard, nearly dragging her at certain points.

Beside Ashley, Katie closed her eyes and concentrated on the music in her headset. She didn't seem all that comfortable with flying, either. But in classic Katie fashion, she was dealing with it by not dealing with it. The music was a perfect distraction.

The adults sat several seats ahead in the roomier first-class cabin. Before take-off, when the attendants had closed the curtain that separated them, Molly had still been able to see them. Then, Mr. and Mrs. Kingsley had been talking quietly together while across from them, Alice read a paperback novel. Her father, of course, hadn't looked up once from his laptop computer.

"Are you all right?" Christina asked now, leaning across the aisle toward pale-faced Ashley.

Without turning her head, Ashley glanced at Christina from the corner of her eye. "Fine," she muttered in an extremely tense voice. "Just fine."

"Poor Ashley," Christina sighed, turning back to Molly. "She's a Libra and they like to be in control. Flying makes them feel totally out of control."

"What sign are you?" Molly asked.

"Aquarius, very idealistic," Christina replied matter-of-factly. "Some say flaky, but that's not so. Aquarians are tuned into things other people don't pay attention to, things like energy levels and the ESP we all have."

Molly nodded. She believed extrasensory perception was possible, but she wasn't sure what all this energy level stuff was about. "What sign is Katie?" she asked.

"Katie is a Scorpio, bossy and stubborn but also very kindhearted and sort of mystical."

"Katie? Mystical?" Molly laughed. "You *are* tuned in to something. No one else would say that."

Christina nodded knowingly. "She just doesn't realize it yet. Katie thinks she's all about facts, but she has another side to her."

Molly stared out the plane window at the mountains of billowing white clouds.

"See any angels?" Christina whispered from the seat beside her.

Molly smiled and continued her cloud gazing. "No, but I wouldn't be surprised. It's so beautiful, isn't it?"

"It sure is," Christina agreed. "I love flying. I think it's one of the most amazing, magical things in the world."

"Tell that to Ashley," Molly said.

"Everyone's different," Christina conceded. "There are twelve signs, all different. And those are just the sun signs. To really figure your signs right you have to know the exact time you were born. That makes a huge difference. Once you know that, the planets all line up differently. You could have your sun sign in Libra, say, but your moon sign and your rising sign could be in Taurus, and you might actually be more of a Taurus than a Libra."

"Sounds complicated."

"It isn't, once you get the hang of it. I'll plot your chart for you, if you like. I've done it lots of times. What sign are you?"

"I have an awful sign," Molly revealed. "Cancer. The crab. Any way you look at it, it's not the greatest."

"Cancer is a very cool sign," Christina disagreed. "Cancerians have this super domestic, conservative side which is totally into family, but hidden below that is a really creative, sometimes wild side. The moon is Cancer's ruling planet, so it makes total sense."

The moon. Molly thought of the Apollo astronauts who had landed on the moon. What must that have been like? It had to have been the most thrilling thing imaginable. And even now, as high up as they were in this 747 jet, there were astronauts even higher in a space shuttle. Those astronauts were circling the moon. "I'd love to go to the moon," she said quietly.

"I believe it. If a Cancerian went to the moon it would be like going home," Christina said. "In a way, it really would." A dreamy look came into her round blue eyes. "I wonder if there are angels in space?"

Molly gazed at her, fascinated by the question. She'd never considered it before. "There must be. Wouldn't you think so?"

"Do you believe in aliens in outer space?" Christina mused. "Do aliens have angels? And, if they do, would they look like alien angels?"

Molly imagined E.T. with wings and a halo. Somehow the picture didn't seem right. Still . . . why shouldn't aliens have angels?

A flight attendant came by offering breakfast. "No, thank you," Molly declined.

"She'd like breakfast," Christina said to the attendant. "And so would I." The smiling attendant set two trays in front of them. "Eat," Christina commanded Molly, nodding at the tray.

"No way. Airline food is so gross." Molly leaned across Christina. "Oh, Miss," she called the flight attendant.

"Yes?" the attendant said, turning to Molly with her practiced smile.

Molly waited for the attendant to come close before speaking. "My father is in first class with three of his associates. I know he would want me to have a first-class meal. He wanted to book my friends and me in first class but it was full."

"I don't know," the attendant said. "It's not the usual thing."

"His name is Ian Morgan," Molly persisted, still smiling. "He flies first class on this airline all the time."

"I'll be right back," the attendant said. As she left, Molly turned to Christina knowingly. "First-class food is so much better. *Everything* in first class is better."

The flight attendant soon returned with four silver-topped trays. She replaced Molly's breakfast, then Christina's, Ashley's, and Katie's. "Enjoy," she said.

"They probably looked him up on their computer or something," Molly said, lifting her tray to reveal a plump omelette, toast, fluffy hash browns, and artfully arranged fruit. "They found out he spends a wad of money on first-class tickets every year, so they want to keep him happy. Isn't this much better?"

Katie leaned across the aisle. "Way to go, Molly," she said. "Real food!"

Molly shot her a thumbs-up.

"Yeah, great food," Christina said, impressed. "I guess when you have a lot of money you can get whatever you want."

Molly began buttering her toast. "Not everything," she said with a shrug. Christina turned her attention to the inviting food on her tray and began eating. As Molly bit into her toast, she looked down at her legs in black velvet leggings. They looked thick to her. All this eating. It was making her heavy. She was eating too much. Everyone kept insisting, but they were going to make her fat. Maybe she could just eat the toast and then mash her other food into small bits and casually roll it into her napkin the way she sometimes used to. She was practically an expert in getting people *not* to notice how little she really ate.

Molly caught herself. This was the kind of thinking that got her in trouble before. She had to stop. She had to think back to everything she was learning in therapy. She closed her eyes to concentrate. *You're thin enough, you're thin enough*, she chanted to herself. *You're thin enough, yurthinnynuf, Yurthinny Nuf.*

Molly opened her eyes and gazed out the window at the clouds. She drew in a sharp breath.

Was this her imagination? Were her eyes playing tricks on her?

Yurthinny Nuf lounged on a cloud, her shimmering purple sequined gown draped gracefully around her large, round form. In her hand was a fat turkey drumstick. Luxuriously, she tossed her black hair back over her round shoulders as she bit rapturously into the drumstick.

"What is it?" Christina asked, following Molly's gaze. "What do you see?"

Molly turned to Christina. "Look. On the cloud," she whispered.

"I don't see anything," Christina said, perplexed.

Molly quickly swiveled her head back to the window. Yurthinny was gone.

* * *

The jet landed at Shannon International Airport. "I can't believe I'm really here," Katie squealed excitedly as they waited in the baggage area for their suitcases to come out.

Still pale and shaken, Ashley stared into space. "It's all right," Molly told her. "You made it. We're here, on solid land."

"At last," Ashley croaked. "But my stomach still thinks it's flying."

When they'd collected their bags, they followed Mr.

Morgan out to where a redheaded chauffeur in a black suit waited, holding a sign with the name Morgan printed on it in big letters. "Come this way," Mr. Morgan told them.

Christina grasped Molly's arm. "A limo!"

"Yeah. Dad always gets a limo when he's traveling," Molly replied.

The group climbed into the spacious, comfortable car. "We'll be able to get a look at Lucky Feather in action very soon," Mr. Morgan was telling Mr. and Mrs. Kingsley and Alice. "He's in the first race at Curragh tomorrow."

"Is it close by?" Mrs. Kingsley asked.

"No, it's on the east coast, in Kildare. Right now, we're in the west. It's a good day's drive from here. After the race, we can bring him to a stable owned by a friend of mine in Connemare, near the castle. There's a chance we might be able to run him at the Limerick Junction Racecourse right here before we fly back."

"How long has the castle been in your family?" Alice asked.

"It's late 1600s. That much we know. The exact date was lost when Oliver Cromwell's men attacked and destroyed the family library. The Beirne's reclaimed it in the late 1700s. Later Beirnes renovated and added different sections right up to the early 1900s, so now, I'm afraid, it's a real jumble of different styles from different eras."

"The Beirnes? Who are they?" Molly asked from her spot in the corner.

"My mother. Your grandmother was Molly Beirne before she married my father," Mr. Morgan explained, glancing out the window. There was something hurried in his voice that gave Molly the idea her father didn't want to talk about his mother. Molly had never met her. She'd died long before Molly was born.

The limo left the city of Limerick. As they drove further out of town, the road became narrower and more winding. Molly peered out the window, mesmerized by the changing landscape. Thin, bony cattle grazed on sloping hillsides edged with slate rock walls. They passed through small towns that made Molly feel as if she'd gone back in time. The buildings were ancient and small and warped with time. The roads were made of cobblestone.

After awhile, the limo began following a winding road on cliffs overlooking the ocean. The day turned cloudy and fat drops of rain slid along the windows. The waves on the choppy ocean below crested in sprays of whitecaps.

Finally, the road began to turn away from the coast. They rode through more small towns and past more pastures until the driver turned down a narrow road. He stopped at an enormous black wrought-iron gate with a swirling pattern of vines.

A small, stout man with white hair, wearing a battered tweed jacket and matching hat, hobbled out of a picturesque thatched cottage behind the gate. He held a ring of keys which he used to unlock the huge gate.

The driver continued down a wide lane lined with bare trees. Their barren, spreading branches danced in the wind and rain.

Molly craned her neck, trying to see what was coming. Suddenly she spied it.

Beirne Castle towered majestically at the end of the wide

lane, looming above them like a castle from a storybook.

High, turreted walls of grayish brown stood at least six stories high. They ran to even higher octagonal towers on each of the four sides. In the center of the front wall, highest of all, about ten stories, was a building with turrets and five large gargoyles leering down at them. Long, narrow windows, more like slits than actual windows, stared at them like dark, unblinking eyes.

"Awesome," Christina murmured.

"Cool," Katie added.

Molly stared, speechless, just as Ashley did. It was so unbelievable that this castle was owned by her family. "Have you ever stayed here before?" she asked her father as they neared the front of the castle.

"Many times," he replied as he, too, stared out the window. "As a boy, I spent a lot of time here."

Molly studied him as he gazed out with a solemn expression. This was the first she'd ever heard of him living in Ireland. She'd always thought he'd lived in England his whole life. He'd gone to boarding school there as a boy. She was certain of that because she'd always thought it sounded completely horrible. How could anyone leave a child on his own with other kids and only teachers to care for him? It seemed so, so heartless.

Yet her father had never complained about it. In fact—unbelievably—he spoke well of the experience. "There's no finer education in the world," he'd said more than once. Molly always winced when he said it. She couldn't help interpreting it as a veiled threat to send her to a girls' boarding school somewhere.

When had he lived in Ireland? And why hadn't he spoken of it up until now?

The limo pulled up to the front door, which was covered by a stone shelter at least twenty feet high. Molly gaped with wonder as she climbed out.

Three wide stone steps led to the arched front door. A ferocious, fire-breathing dragon was carved in either side of the heavy wooden door. "Look at that," said Ashley pointing over her head. A laughing court jester peered down at them, his spreading arms fashioned so that he appeared to be holding up the roof of the shelter.

"Look at this," Katie said, pointing to a corner where a stone woman in an elaborate headdress solemnly stared back at them.

"Here's her husband," Christina pointed out, nodding toward a stone man dressed in medieval garb and standing regally in the opposite corner.

The heavy door creaked open and a small, wrinkled woman with gray hair appeared. "Welcome, Ian . . . er . . . Mr. Morgan," she said warmly in a rich Irish brogue. "Everything has been prepared."

"Thank you, Mrs. Loughlin," Mr. Morgan said with a smile, leading the way into the castle.

Molly and the others followed him in. "Wow!" Katie murmured, staring up as they walked into the main hallway. Dim light filtered through the narrow stained-glass windows high above them. "This hallway is as big as my whole house. The ceiling here must be three stories high."

"Shall I show everyone to their rooms?" Mrs. Loughlin asked Mr. Morgan. He nodded and Mrs. Loughlin beckoned for everyone to follow her up a curved flight of wide stairs in the center of the gigantic hall.

Mrs. Loughlin led them down a shadowy hall with a stone floor. She paused in front of a wooden door and opened it with a creak. "The warmer rooms are on this floor," she said. "Although the castle is large, not all the rooms are heated or have been kept up as well. Perhaps the young ladies would like to share this one."

Molly stepped inside and saw that the room had a large, gray stone fireplace and two lavishly quilted double beds. The green, gold, and white quilts on the beds matched the tassled canopies overhead. At the end of each bed lay identical blankets woven in a gorgeous blend of lavender and deep green. Molly ran her hands along the impossibly soft wool.

"Beautiful, aren't they," Mrs. Loughlin said. "They're handwoven by women on the Aran Islands, not far from here. They raise their own sheep and make their own natural dyes."

"Awesome," Christina commented, stepping into the room.

Katie and Ashley entered the room behind Christina while Mrs. Loughlin moved on, taking the others to their rooms.

The four girls turned in circles, taking in the high-ceilinged room with its heavy black beams.

"Look at this writing desk," cried Katie, clapping her hands with delight at the sight of a heavy marble-topped mahogany desk sitting to the right of the fireplace. "What a place to write my story."

Ashley ran her delicate, manicured hand along the

crisp linen hand towels set out beside a gleaming white pitcher and bowl on a stand by the door. "I bet this is real Irish linen," she said, impressed. She lifted one of the four sparkling water glasses by the pitcher and turned it, admiring its sharply cut edges. "This is probably real Waterford crystal, too."

"How do you know about all that stuff?" Katie asked, spreading her notebook and pens out on the desk. "Waterford and Irish linen?"

"Mom likes it. She always shows it to me in catalogs. I like it, too—a lot. But it's expensive."

Molly smiled. Expensive things didn't impress her. But this room impressed her. It was so perfect, as if it had been sitting here, just waiting for them to arrive. It was like a room from a book—or a dream.

She wandered to one of the windows. It was separated into squares by heavy leading between every pane. She looked out through the thick, somewhat wavery glass at the back of the castle. Below her was a very large field enclosed by a stonework fence with side-by-side hexagons embedded in it. Molly could easily imagine knights jousting in that open, level field. Only a low stone bench in the middle of the field spoiled the effect. She imagined several court pages scurrying out to move it out of the way of the charging knights.

Beyond the field and the stone enclosure was a wild jumble of bare trees and some browning greenery which sloped down sharply. Beyond that, Molly could see the turbulent, blue-black ocean churning about the cliff.

"What a view," Ashley said, coming up beside her. "I wonder if there's a way down to the ocean."

"It's stopped raining. Want to explore?" Molly suggested.

"Sure," Ashley said enthusiastically. They turned to Katie, who had settled in at the desk and was tapping the blank page of her notebook with the cap end of her pen, already deep in thought. "Want to explore?"Ashley repeated.

"Huh?" Katie said, startled. "Oh, uh, no. I want to write about the castle. You guys go without me. Let me know if you find anything . . . mysterious."

"How about you?" Molly asked Christina, who sat on the edge of one of the beds looking curiously blank.

"No, thanks," she said. "All of a sudden I feel weird."

"It's just jet lag," Molly said, resetting the time on her dainty silver watch. "Changing time zones messes up your sleep cycle. Sleep and you'll feel better."

"That's funny, I feel wide awake. Almost super awake," Ashley said.

"Jet lag hits everyone differently," Molly said. "You'll probably feel it later and crash. That's what happened to me last time we went to France."

"France. Wow!" Ashley sighed.

"Let's try to get down to the ocean," Molly suggested as they left the room and walked down the hallway.

"Do you know where the back door is?" Ashley asked as they reached the bottom of the stone stairway.

Molly looked around. The hallway opened into rooms on both sides. "I have no idea. Let's just hunt around until we find it."

They entered a room to the right. A long room with many high windows, it had a long, formal dining table in its center. At one end they spied narrow winding stone steps. Following the steps down led to a dark, window-less room with an immense fireplace. They pushed through a door on the far side of the room and stepped out into the damp afternoon.

"I don't see a path anywhere," Ashley said, looking around. They walked along the edge of the stone fence, gazing down at the tangle of dense shrubbery below. "The ocean is obviously at the bottom of this slope, but I just don't see how we can get there."

Molly scanned the area and finally saw a narrow opening in the bare bushes. "There. Maybe that's the path."

They climbed over the fence and carefully moved through the branches of the hedge. Sure enough, a dirt path led away through a tangle of shrubs. As they followed it, the trail got steeper and narrower. Some of the bushes they passed had thorns that almost seemed to reach out and grab at them with sharp, spindly fingers.

One caught at Molly's silver watch. "You don't get this," she said as she yanked her wrist free. The watch had been a gift from her parents for her thirteenth birthday.

Molly's parents always gave her spectacular gifts on her birthdays. Along with the watch they'd given her her very own cellular phone. But the watch was the most precious gift of all to Molly. It had belonged to her grandmother on her father's side. Although she'd never known her grandmother, Molly knew the watch was special to her father. She could see it in his eyes when he looked at it. An unusual soft light crept into them then.

"Molly," he'd said at the time, "this was my mother's, and I think she'd have wanted you to have it."

"What was she like?" Molly had asked him.

"Oh, well, she died long ago," he'd replied. "It's hard to remember." Yet, Molly was sure—she could see it in his eyes, in the softening of his face—that the watch meant a lot to him. And he'd given it to her. It was possibly the warmest gesture of love she'd ever received from him.

The girls continued beating a path through the branches and underbrush. Round, brown burrs stuck to Molly's velvet leggings and caught in her long braid. "I wonder if this is worth it," she said to Ashley.

"The ocean can't be *too* far away," Ashley said optimistically as she pulled her foot free of some dead vines on the ground.

After ten minutes, the land flattened and the bushes and trees ended. They weren't at the ocean, but at a graveyard.

From all appearances, the graveyard had been abandoned for years. No flowers or wreaths decorated any of the timeworn, lichen-covered headstones, which all sloped to the right as if buffeted by centuries of steady wind. The uniformity of thin stone tablets was interrupted occasionally by more elaborate monuments—a Celtic cross, adorned with its circle; a statue of St. Patrick with the banished snakes of Ireland writhing under his sandals; various saints and angels.

Molly was about to step into the cemetery when Ashley grasped her arm and pulled her back.

"What?" Molly gasped.

"Over there," Ashley whispered urgently. "A leprechaun."

6

Molly followed Ashley's shocked gaze to the far corner of the graveyard. Confused, she scanned the area. All she saw was a six-foot-high stone angel.

Waves of stone curls framed the angel's smooth gray face. She knelt on one knee, her huge wings spread behind her. Her two arms held a large, scalloped stone bowl.

"I don't see a—" Molly began, but then caught herself short as a small head suddenly popped up from behind the angel's head. It belonged to a person small enough to be a child, but the eyes peering out of the face belonged to an adult.

Molly got a clearer look as the small figure crept out onto the angel's immense, celestial wing. The person wore a green tunic with a thick brown bag attached to a belt and small, dark brown boots. He or she—it was hard to tell which—had short, bright red hair. The figure clutched the wing with small hands and pushed with his or her knees until he or she was at the very tip of the curved wing.

Looking back at Ashley with a wonder-filled expression, Molly was too stunned to speak. Of course she'd *heard* of leprechauns, the small, magical elves of the Irish woods, but she'd never actually believed in them. But this little person certainly *looked* like a leprechaun.

"Let's try to get a better look," Ashley suggested, her voice a breathless whisper.

Crouching low, the girls scurried from headstone to headstone as quietly as they could manage. In a short time, they were hiding behind a headstone very near to the angel. Up close, it was clear from the softly wrinkled features and delicate hands that the leprechaun was female.

"What do we do now?" Molly whispered.

"I don't know," Ashley admitted. "Should we grab her and try to get wishes or gold or something?"

Molly checked the leprechaun. She now sat on the wing and was rummaging for something in the brown cloth bag she had tied to her belt. It seemed sort of rude to just leap out and grab her the way people often did in tales about leprechauns.

Just then, the leprechaun began waving her arms wildly. "Oh! Oh! Oh, dear! Oh!" she cried as her legs flew up and she toppled backwards onto the ground.

Startled, the girls instinctively jumped up and ran to help her. "Are you all right?" Ashley asked, as she took hold of one childlike arm.

The woman's deep green eyes darted back and forth between the girls in alarm.

"We saw you fall," Molly explained. "Are you hurt?"

The woman sat up and brushed dried brown grass

from her green tunic. "I'm quite all right," she said brusquely in a thick brogue. "Who are you girls? What are you doing out here? I thought I was all alone, I did."

"We're staying up at the castle," Ashley spoke first. "I'm Ashley and this is—"

"Molly Morgan," the small woman said softly, locking Molly in a steady gaze.

"How did you know my name?" Molly asked.

"And," the woman said, getting to her feet, "you must be the daughter of . . . no . . . must be the *grand*daughter of Molly Beirne Morgan, are you not?"

"That's me," Molly admitted. "How did you know?"

The small woman chuckled. "How could I *not* know? You're the double of the dear woman."

"I am?"

"Yes, except—now that I look at you—you're a bit too thin to be her exact duplicate. But, with a few more pounds you could be her twin." The woman broke into a wide, warm smile, her green eyes fairly twinkling. "Mrs. Fitzlagen is my name, by the way."

Hearing Mrs. Fitzlagen's name suddenly made Molly feel very foolish. Her name made her seem quite real. She was a Mrs.—someone's wife. She'd known her grandmother, though she must have been quite young when she knew her. But she certainly was not a leprechaun at all. She was simply an extremely short old woman.

Molly gazed hard at Mrs. Fitzlagen, trying to calculate how old she was in relationship to her grandmother. She lifted her arm to show her silver watch. "This belonged to my grandmother."

Mrs. Fitzlagen took Molly's wrist with strong, but very

soft, hands. "So, 'tis her own watch," she murmured in a reverent voice. "I'd know it anywhere. You're a lucky girl to have been presented with such a gift."

"What was she like, my grandmother?" Molly wanted to know.

"Well, besides looking almost exactly like you, she was a dear girl. Lovely. Kind." Mrs. Fitzlagen folded her arms and cocked her head. Studying Molly for another moment, she shook her head fondly.

"Little Molly Beirne's granddaughter, eh? How time flitters by on angel wings."

"Uh . . . speaking of angel wings," Ashley ventured. "Why were you . . . um . . . climbing on . . ."

The woman chuckled again and blushed. She bent and picked up her bag. "Ah, you caught me in the act. You've uncovered my little secret."

For one whimsical moment, Molly thought the woman was about to reveal that she was, indeed, a leprechaun and pull a pot of gold from her bag. Instead, she produced something that looked like a small, pale yellow paper bag of sugar.

"Cement?" Ashley read the label in a confused tone.

"Aye," the woman said, nodding. "I have a bit of a problem on my hands." Her green eyes brightened. "Perhaps you could help me with it."

"All right," Molly agreed quickly, imagining wishes granted in return for kindly behavior. What would she wish for? The chance to go to Space Camp, for starters.

The woman gazed up at the stone angel towering over her. "See that crack there at the top of the wing?"

Molly and Ashley looked and immediately noticed a

jagged crack running from the tip all the way to the outer edge of the wing about halfway down.

"If that crack isn't patched, it will spread. When water gets in it this winter, it will freeze and push the crack open wider. By spring, the top of that wing will have cracked right off. I thought I could crawl up and then mix the cement to patch it. But, as you saw, I lost my balance. I can't reach it from the ground, though. It makes for quite a difficulty."

Molly saw what the woman meant. The angel was so lovely. It would be a shame if its wing really did crack off. "I think I can reach it," she offered. "Just tell me what to do."

The woman quickly took a small bowl, a canteen, and a spatula from her pack. She poured cement into the bowl, then added water from the canteen and stirred with the spatula. She handed the wet cement to Molly. "Dab it in gently," she instructed. "You don't need too much."

Molly did her best to patch the crack with small bits of cement. It wasn't as easy as she'd thought, though. The cement dribbled down her arms and wouldn't stay where she put it. Carefully, Molly took off her silver watch and rested it in the stone angel's empty bowl.

When she was done, Molly stepped back and frowned at her work. Cement oozed from the crack and ran down the sides. "Sort of a messy job," she said apologetically.

The little woman turned to Ashley. "Give me a boost up, would you, love?" she requested. "I can do the finishing work."

Ashley grasped the woman around the waist and lifted

her. Though petite herself, Ashley had no difficulty holding Mrs. Fitzlagen as she braced her little feet against the wing. Taking the spatula from Molly, she dabbed at the cement, scraping off small bits and smoothing it until the wing was once again a seamless whole.

"Wow, you're good at that," Molly commented as Ashley gently set the elderly woman down beside the angel.

The woman beamed proudly. "It's my specialty. I've been doing it for years, more years than you can imagine. I hate to see these old monuments crumble, especially the angels. I am so fond of them in particular."

"You're really talented," Ashley commented.

"Do you get paid a lot for restoring these?" Molly asked.

"Paid a lot?" the woman guffawed. "No, my dear. Not at all. I don't get paid a penny. I do it for love." She peered hard at Molly. "Forgive me, but you look so much like your dear grandmother, I can't get over it."

"Tell me more about her," Molly asked, hungry for every detail about the grandmother she'd never known.

"She was so sweet, but not simpering. She was bold and full of fun. And very adventurous. She died so young. It was truly a loss to those who loved her. A terrible loss for them."

"How did she die?" Molly asked.

"It was a terrible pneumonia that took her." Mrs. Fitzlagen looked up at the overcast, ever-darkening sky. "I think of her as living, still, among the stars. A great love she had for the stars and planets. Always looking up, wondering about what was up there."

Ashley put her hand on Molly's shoulder. "Just like you," she said in a low voice.

As Molly nodded in agreement, the sky opened, unleashing a torrent of rain. "Oh, good heavens!" cried Mrs. Fitzlagen, tossing her cement, spatula, and bowl back into her bag.

Along with Mrs. Fitzlagen, Molly and Ashley dashed across the graveyard back toward the dirt path they'd come down. For someone so small and old, Mrs. Fitzlagen ran with astonishing speed. She got ahead of the girls and scurried on into the trees.

Just as Ashley and Molly reached the woods, Molly realized something was missing. She'd left her silver watch in the stone angel's bowl. If she didn't go back for it, the bowl would fill up and the watch would be ruined. "I'll be right back," she told Ashley. "Keep going. I'll catch up with you."

Molly hurried back to the angel monument, weaving her way through the headstones. But when she reached the angel, the watch was no longer in the bowl.

I know I put it there, she thought, frantically checking around the angel's bent arms and in the stone folds of her gown. *Where could it have gone?*

Had it bounced out of the bowl?

She couldn't stay out here forever looking for it, but she refused to lose it.

As rain soaked her clothing, Molly dropped to her knees and searched around the base of the angel, groping through handfuls of thick, drenched grass. Each time her hands came up muddy and empty. She crawled forward steadily as biting rain pelted her unmercifully.

That was when she saw the inscription under the angel.

This angel marked the grave of . . . Molly Morgan.

7

"That must have been so weird," Christina said that night as the girls basked in the warmth of the cozy fire banked in their bedroom fireplace. "Seeing your own name on a grave," she mused, her eyes glowing in the firelight.

"It was," Molly told her friends. "It was eerie." She tucked her feet under her green flannel nightgown. "I can't believe I found my grandmother's grave like that."

She'd finally had to give up the search for her watch. The rain kept beating down on her, and Ashley couldn't wait any longer. Besides, seeing her own name on the grave had disconcerted her so much that she could no longer think about the watch. It was like looking at her own grave. It had made her want to turn and run—which she did.

She and Ashley ran the rest of the way back to the castle in the pouring rain. Wringing wet, Molly had commandeered one of the huge old-fashioned bathrooms and drawn a long, soothing bath in its funny claw-footed bathtub. Now it was wonderfully comforting to be sitting here by the fire Mrs. Loughlin had set for them.

"You never did find your watch, though, did you?" Ashley said as she lay across a fat pillow on the floor.

"No. I'm going back to look for it again. It belonged to my grandmother," Molly said. "I've got to get it back. It's . . . irreplaceable." As she spoke the words, the reality of it struck her hard. How odd to have something that couldn't be replaced. This was the first time she'd ever really experienced such a thing. How many times had her mother crooned, "Don't worry, darling, we'll buy you another," when some beloved toy had been broken beyond repair or irretrievably lost? No wonder Molly had always assumed everything could be replaced—and almost everything could. But not this.

Katie held her hands out to let the fire warm them. "Mmmmm, the fire feels good," she said, shutting her eyes. At night, the dampness and chill seemed to creep from outside through the stone walls into the castle. If this was the heated part, Molly was glad they were here. She couldn't imagine how uncomfortable it must be in the unheated part. The fire helped a lot, and thank goodness someone always made sure it blazed welcomingly.

Opening her eyes, Katie turned to Molly. "It's sort of mysterious, losing your grandmother's watch right at her very grave. Don't you think?"

"That's just your writer's mind at work," Ashley laughed.

"*I* think it's interesting, too," Christina agreed with Katie. "I bet it's more than a coincidence," she added meaningfully.

"Oh, man," Katie groaned, waving her hands as if to

push Christina away. "Don't start with that 'more than a coincidence,' stuff. I'm sorry I said anything about it. I bet the answer is simple. That weird Mrs. Fitz-whatever snatched your watch."

"No!" Ashley objected. "She was a sweet old lady, Katie, not a pickpocket!"

Katie shrugged. "Who else could have taken it? And why did she disappear into the woods so fast?"

Molly and Ashley exchanged glances. Mrs. Fitzlagen *had* completely disappeared. There had been no sign of her on the path at all. She couldn't have run very fast on those short legs of hers. "Maybe she took a side path that led to her home," Ashley speculated.

"Or maybe she hid behind a tree until you passed," Katie countered cynically. She went to her bed and opened her suitcase. She took out the black-and-white notebook which she used as a journal. "Day one in Ireland," she said as she wrote. "Pouring rain. Molly had her watch snatched. But the castle is so cool. I can easily imagine ghosts everywhere."

"Don't say that," Ashley said with a shiver.

"She's right, though," Christina said, sitting forward. "I feel presences here."

"Don't start with that!" Katie barked automatically. "I mean it!"

"You're the one who started it," Christina reminded her calmly. "You said you thought there were ghosts here."

"Yeah, but *I* was just trying to be spooky," Katie said, rolling her eyes. "*You* mean it!"

"I *do* mean it," Christina insisted. "I feel something. I feel that there are unseen forces here."

"I believe you," Ashley said. "Your feelings are right so often."

"Who could be here?" Katie scoffed. "Some clanky old knight?"

Molly got up and walked to the window. The rain had stopped, but the trees were whipped by a violent wind. The nearly-full moon lit the turbulent ocean beyond the trees. What presences could there be in this old castle? she wondered. Ghosts? Leprechauns? Brownies? Was it her grandmother's spirit that haunted this huge, damp building?

Soon, the combination of jet lag and a long day caught up with them, and one by one, the girls straggled to bed, Christina and Katie in one, Ashley and Molly in the other.

Molly tossed restlessly, half-asleep, half-awake, until finally exhaustion overtook her. But her racing mind couldn't rest.

She dreamed that she was walking out of the castle into the night. She found her way down to the ocean and stepped out onto a jetty. The wild ocean rose up on both sides, spraying her with a salty mist. The moon was a gigantic orange ball hanging low over the water.

In her dream, Molly gazed up and saw three dark figures silhouetted against the moon. Three winged figures. Angels.

She walked to the end of the jetty, raised her arms longingly, and felt herself lifted off her feet. She was floating high into the sky. She was floating to the moon. The moon. Home. She had the strongest sensation that the light of the moon was pulling her up, bringing her home. She tried to step forward, to hurry the journey.

As she stepped, she lost the serene balance which had kept her floating so effortlessly. She panicked, kicking the air frantically. Her arms flailed in a desperate attempt to grasp something real to hold onto. And then, suddenly, she pitched forward and began to plummet headfirst down toward the churning, black ocean.

"Help me!" she screamed. "Somebody help me!"

Immediately, a hand grasped her arm. "Molly! Molly! Wake up!"

Molly's eyes snapped open. She was sitting up. In the dying firelight she saw Ashley's concerned face. "You were dreaming," Ashley told her. "It was just a dream."

Molly blinked hard, willing herself awake.

"What did you dream?" Katie asked from her bed where Christina still slumbered beside her. "You screamed for help."

"I did?" Molly asked. "I screamed out loud?"

"Yes. That's why we're awake," Ashley told her.

"Oh, sorry," Molly said. "I'm okay now. I dreamed I was falling out of the sky."

"Scary," Katie sympathized.

The girls went back to sleep. Molly turned on her side and this time she had no dreams.

*   *   *

The next morning the sky was a deep, vibrant blue. "The stormy weather yesterday blew all the clouds out to sea," Mrs. Loughlin commented as she bustled about, serving a huge Irish breakfast of hot oatmeal, juice, fried eggs, ham, and biscuits on the long, formal table in the dining room. Molly gazed distastefully at the abundant breakfast spread. She ate a small bowl of oatmeal and passed on the rest. Christina cast a stern look her way, but Molly's father didn't seem to notice. He was busy studying something on his laptop.

"According to the Dublin newspapers, Lucky Feather is the favorite to win the race this afternoon," Mr. Morgan reported, looking up at the others.

"You get that from your computer?" Mr. Kingsley asked, eyebrows raised.

"Yes, I'm plugged into the phone jack over there and now I'm online to read periodicals from all over the world," Mr. Morgan explained.

"Amazing," Alice commented, reaching for the silver coffeepot.

After breakfast, the adults all piled into the waiting limo taking them to the Curragh Racecourse in County Kildare. "You listen to Mrs. Loughlin," Mrs. Kingsley said to the girls as she climbed inside. "We'll be back tomorrow night."

"Have a good trip," Molly said to her father as he got into the limo.

Her father nodded distractedly. "Yes, thanks. I'm sure we will." With a quick smile, he shut the door.

"What do you want to do now?" Katie asked as they watched the limo drive away down the wide, tree-lined road.

"I want to look for my watch," Molly replied. She left the front entranceway and stepped onto the still-wet grass. The others followed her as she went around the side of the castle.

"Awesome," Christina commented at the sight of a

stone knight carved into the corner of the castle.

They went over the stone wall back down into the trees and thick underbrush. "I still say that midget woman nabbed it," Katie maintained. "This isn't going to get us anywhere."

"Think positively," Ashley told her. "Now that it's a nice day I bet we *do* find it."

With Molly in the lead, they found their way back to the graveyard. "This spot is alive with energy," Christina said, wandering out among the stones.

"Alive!" Katie yelped. "Do you have to use that word?"

"No, really. Can't you feel the power surging here?" She stood with her arms extended and her eyes shut.

"Oh, you feel power spots everywhere. Anyway, stop it," Katie said. "You're giving me the creeps."

"There's nothing creepy about it," Christina said, opening her eyes. "I don't mean there are spirits here. There are just some natural spots in nature where universal energy pools and collects. Haven't you read about all the people who go to that town in Arizona just to experience the natural energy vortex?"

"No," Katie said bluntly.

"Well, there is a place like that. And I think this is another one. The people who started this cemetery probably sensed it. That's why they put graves here."

"Come on, help me look," Molly called to her friends. She was looking in the stone folds of the angel's gown. She just couldn't believe that nice Mrs. Fitzlagen had taken it. It had to be here. It just had to be. Her friends joined her, each one searching a different section of the angel. Ashley scooped twigs and leaves from the angel's rainwater-filled bowl. Katie pored through the angel's curls with her fingers. Christina got to her knees and started crawling around the base of the angel. Suddenly, she looked up sharply, her blue eyes wide.

"What?" Molly asked, noticing her shocked expression. "What's wrong?"

"Look at this," Christina said quietly. She pointed to a patch of mud just to the right of the stone angel.

"I don't see anything," Katie said.

Molly bent and studied the mud patch. "It's a footprint," she murmured.

"A bare footprint," Ashley added.

"And there are more of them leading down that path," Katie pointed out, nodding at a wet dirt path leading away from the angel monument. Molly narrowed her eyes and inspected the path. Katie was right. Bare footprints went all the way down the path as far as she could see until the path disappeared into the trees.

As one, the girls turned and looked at the bare foot of the angel that peeked out from under her gown. Her foot was roughly the same size as the footprints.

Slowly, they looked up at the angel's serene face. Then they looked at one another. "Naaaah!" they said in one voice. "Naaaah."

8

Overcome with curiosity, the girls followed the trail of bare footprints down the path. "The prints are so clear," Molly noted, peering at the well-defined prints sunk heavily into the mud. "Whoever made them was heavy."

"Heavy as a statue," Christina said ominously.

"Don't be crazy," Katie scolded. "Statues don't walk around."

They continued down the path as it sloped through the bare trees. At places where the bushes tangled wildly with one another, they lost the trail but were able to pick it up further on.

After awhile, Molly became aware of the sound of crashing waves in the distance. She picked up her pace, anxious to see the ocean. Just as she became aware that the air had picked up a salty scent, the path widened. The girls stepped out onto a rocky ledge. Looking down, they saw they'd have to climb down a steep, rocky slope to get to the beach below. "No more prints," Katie noted. "This is the end of them."

"Let's go down anyway," Molly suggested. "I've been wanting to find the beach."

The trip down was difficult. Rocks tumbled loose under their feet, throwing them off balance. Ashley slid and grasped a low-growing, scrubby shrub to break her fall. Christina opted to scoot all the way down on her bottom, while Katie cautiously backed down, hanging onto whatever rock or plant was available. Molly found it easiest to move sideways, steadying her bottom foot before bringing her top foot down to meet it. In about ten minutes more or less, they'd all made it to the bottom.

"Look!" Ashley cried, peering out over the wet sand. "I see the footprints again. They lead all the way into the water."

Excitedly, they ran across the soft brown sand, following the footprints to the undulating shoreline.

"Wait a minute," Katie said, tensing. "Something is very weird here."

Molly gazed at her anxiously. "What?"

"Can't you see?" Katie exclaimed. "The tide isn't washing the prints away. It washes in and out over the prints but they're still there."

"You're right," Ashley concurred, squatting to get a better look at the prints. "It's as if they've become part of the earth, like a fossil or something."

Shutting her eyes, Christina bent and carefully placed her fingers into one of the prints as the foaming white surf swept over it.

"*Now* what are you doing?" Katie asked impatiently. "Your shoes are getting soaked."

Christina opened her eyes. "I'm feeling how it feels."

"How *does* it feel?" Molly asked.

Straightening, Christina rolled her eyes to the side as she thought. "It feels like energy from the earth traveled into me."

"How can you tell that?" Katie challenged her.

"It's a feeling," Christina replied. "How can you tell if you're feeling sick or weak or strong? You *feel* it."

Katie nodded. It was hard to argue with Christina. *Something* was going on. As wave after wave failed to erase the footprints, that much was clear.

Molly shivered as a cold, wet wind whipped her long French braid. Gazing out to sea, she saw ominous black storm clouds rolling in from the horizon and gradually blotting out the wispy white clouds billowing across the crystal blue sky. "They sure have rotten weather here," she commented.

"Let's follow these prints," Ashley suggested, already moving along the shore.

The footprints stayed on the shoreline for several yards, then moved on up the beach toward the majestic, soaring rock cliffs that lined the shore. As the girls followed them, the beach grew narrower until there was only a six-foot shelf of rocky sand between the cliffs and the ocean. The water lapped at their feet, splashing up onto their shoes and the bottoms of their pants.

Abruptly, the footprints stopped. "Now what?" Katie asked.

Molly shrugged helplessly. What could have happened to the prints? There were no footprints turning back in the opposite direction. As one, the girls raised their eyes up the rock wall of the cliff. Whoever made these prints could only have climbed up. But it was impossible. The choppy, cracked rock wall was too steep and sheer.

Unless, of course, the print-maker had flown.

Molly was considering this possibility when something in the rock wall caught her attention. A wide, vertical crack in the rock appeared to be flickering with an uneven, wavering light. "Hey, look at this," she said.

The girls huddled together and studied the crack. "It's not a reflection," Katie said, looking back over her shoulder. "The sun isn't bright enough anymore."

"Maybe it's some metallic stone inside the rock," Ashley speculated.

"It almost looks like a candle," Christina considered. "But that's impossible."

Molly put her face up to the gritty, cold rock and studied the crack critically. It was obviously very deep. The light was coming from way inside it. "I bet I could squeeze through this opening," she said. "If I sucked in my breath, I could do it."

"What if you got stuck?" Katie worried.

"I wouldn't," Molly insisted. "Face it. I'm thin enough to do it."

"Not me," Christina said. "I couldn't."

"No," Molly agreed. "I bet Ashley could, though."

Ashley bit her lip. "I don't like small spaces," she said. "I guess I'm a little claustrophobic."

"Okay," Molly said. "I'm going to try it, though. I want to see what's in there."

"Careful," Katie cautioned anxiously as Molly slid her legs into the crack. She kept pushing forward until her entire body was inside the crack.

She stopped as her shoulders suddenly became wedged between the sides. Panic seized her fiercely and unexpectedly. Why had she gone in here? Was she crazy? Squirming desperately, Molly tried to free herself. But the more she wriggled, the more tightly she felt stuck in place. "Help!" she called out to the slab of daylight she could still see. "I'm stuck."

She heard her friends talking, but couldn't make out their words. Even if they tried to help her, what could they possibly do?

"Help!" Molly screamed, flailing her legs. As she kicked, she realized she couldn't feel any rock around her feet. Could the opening be wider there? She kicked again until she felt a rock lip. Hooking her foot around it, she pulled, straining every muscle.

"Aaaahhhh!" she cried out as her shoulders came free of the stone wall. Scrambling as fast as she could, Molly tumbled into an open space. "Oomph!" She hit the hard floor, knocked breathless for a moment.

When she recovered her breath, she immediately found the source of the flickering light. A tin lantern sat propped on a stone ledge several feet above her head. The stub of a candle burned within it.

Molly got to her feet, brushing off the seat of her pants. All around she heard the dripping of water. The place was so wet and cold it sent a shiver through her. Small rivulets of water trickled down the craggy stone walls.

Clearly, someone had been there before her. The lantern wasn't the only indication. A line of tall, greenish glass bottles sat in a row on the floor, shimmering softly in the lantern's glow.

A scratching sound nearby made Molly tense. It sounded like nails on stone. Claws! Was it some animal? Was she about to be trapped in here with some, some creature with sharp claws?

Bats lived in caves, didn't they?

The sound was definitely getting louder. It was coming from the entrance to the cave, the one she'd just squeezed through.

A dark form appeared in the moving half-light. Molly backed against the wall, squeezing herself flat against it.

"Ashley!" she gasped as Ashley's face appeared in the opening.

"I broke a nail," Ashley complained, stretching her hand out in front of her. "Are you okay? We heard you yell for help."

Molly let out a sigh of relief. "I got stuck, but I made it through." She went to the tunnel entrance and helped pull Ashley the rest of the way through. Molly saw that her friend was pale and panting.

"Why did you come through?" she asked. "You're claustrophobic."

"I had to," Ashley snapped with uncharacteristic irritability. "I'm the only one who's small enough."

"Thank you," Molly said sincerely. She was touched that Ashley had come despite her fears.

"It's a little better in here, anyway," Ashley observed, wiping dirty sweat from her forehead. "What is this place?"

"I don't know, but someone's been here. I wonder how long that lantern's been burning."

"There's something up there next to the lantern," Ashley observed, pointing. "A book or something."

Molly saw it too—a brown leather book about the size of her hand. It was inlaid with gold trim, which glimmered tantalizingly in the candlelight.

"I bet I could reach it," Molly said speculatively. She jumped and her fingertips brushed the book's smooth surface. Her second jump nearly unsettled the lamp, which flickered ominously.

"Careful," Ashley warned in a slightly shaky voice. "We don't want to be stuck here in the dark. That would really skeeve me out."

"Okay. I'll be more careful," Molly assured her. On the third jump, she slapped the book, knocking it off the ledge.

It tumbled past her and fell open facedown at her feet. As she knelt to pick it up, she froze, staring not at the book, but at something on the ground beside it.

"Ashley," she said in a low, urgent voice. "Look."

On the floor of the cave were more of the bare footprints they'd followed.

9

Molly and Ashley simply stared at one another in astonishment. What was going on? Who or what was making these prints?

"What is this place?" Ashley asked again. She picked up one of the tall green glass bottles and held it up to the light. "There's paper in here," she observed.

Molly studied the bottle in Ashley's hands. A brownish piece of paper was rolled up like a small scroll inside it. "A message?" she wondered.

Ashley tipped the bottle, but the message was too loosely wrapped to come out easily. She tried wiggling her fingers into the neck of the bottle. Still, she was unable to pull the message out. "We'll have to break it to get this out," she decided.

"I don't want to break glass in here," Molly said as she slid the small, leather book securely into the back waistband of her pants in order to free her hands. "Let me try." As Molly reached out for the bottle, a burbling sound at the tunnel entrance caught her attention.

Looking up sharply, she saw a gush of water rush into the cave. "Ashley," she cried, alarmed. "Look!"

Whirling around, Ashley paled at the sight of the water. "Oh, no!" Ashley cried. "The tide must be coming in. How could it have come up so fast?"

"I don't know," Molly said, fighting down panic. "I've heard of places where the tide comes up super fast. Let's get out of here!"

She could dimly hear the urgent sound of voices yelling outside. It had to be Christina and Katie calling to them. Another gush of water whooshed into the cave, spilling down like a waterfall and splashing them as it hit the rock floor. "Let's go," Molly urged Ashley.

Ashley gripped her arm. "What if the water rushes in while we're wedged in that tunnel? We'll drown!"

Molly forced herself to keep thinking and not give in to panic. "We'll hold our breath until the wave passes. That should give us enough time to get out."

Despite her logical words, Molly recalled being wedged in the cave at her shoulders. What if she couldn't make it forward through that tight squeeze this time? What if the water flooded over her and she couldn't move? She might be stuck there as wave after wave hit her. And if she was stuck, Ashley would be stuck behind her. "You'd better go first," she told Ashley.

"Why me?" Ashley gasped, backing up.

"Because you're smaller. I don't want you to get stuck behind me."

"Stuck!" Ashley shrieked.

Outside, the muffled yelling grew more frantic. Christina and Katie must be urging them to get out of there. "The water must not reach as high as the lantern," Molly reasoned. "Otherwise it wouldn't still be burning. It won't cover us completely. We'll float up with it."

"Oh, just great! We'll be stuck here floating in freezing water," Ashley said, dancing around nervously in the small pool forming on the floor. "I don't know how long I can tread water. I'm not a great swimmer."

Molly stared at the water that now trickled in, the calm before the next rush. "We can't stand around talking. Once the water passes the tunnel entrance we won't be able to get out at all."

"I can't do it," Ashley insisted, her hand pressed to her chest.

"We have to," Molly said firmly.

Ashley began to quiver from head to foot. "I can't. I can't face it. It was hard enough to crawl through before. I can't do it again with sea water washing over me. Katie and Christina will think of something. They'll help us."

"They can't," Molly reminded her. "They can't fit through."

"They'll get help," Ashley insisted.

"There was no one on the beach," Molly said, folding her arms tightly to ward off the cold and her own terror. "They won't be able to get back to the castle in time."

Molly jumped away from the dark tunnel entrance as another wave washed through it, spilling onto the floor in a foaming swirl. Each wave seemed more forceful than the one before it. Ashley's panic began to seep into Molly's own fragile, forced calm. "I don't think I can do it, either," she said as yet another wave crashed into the cave.

Ashley looked at her, pale and wide-eyed. "This is it," she said in a small, reedy voice. "We're stuck."

"No," Molly said with new resolve. "If we don't do something, we'll die." Molly wasn't about to accept defeat. She realized she had to be strong for herself and for Ashley. She had to think of something. It was up to her. Ashley had been brave enough to crawl in, now it was up to her, Molly, to get her out.

"I suppose we could climb up on this rock for awhile," Ashley said, looking up at the glistening black stone around them. There were small niches where a hand or foot might fit, but there wasn't much to grip. It would be grueling work. "Even if we climbed, though, we couldn't hold on long enough to do any real good."

As Ashley spoke, Molly turned to the sound of something scuffling within the tunnel. "Mrs. Fitzlagen!" she cried as the small woman appeared.

As Molly and Ashley helped her through, another gush of water poured in, soaking them in its icy spray. "Ah! Good heavens!" the woman cried, wiping water from her face.

"How did you find us?" Ashley asked.

"I was collecting mussels when I saw two girls running up the beach. In a panic, they were. But there's no time for storytelling now. Follow me." Mrs. Fitzlagen hurried on her tiny legs to a dark, shadowy corner of the cave. Here, the ceiling rose higher than in any other spot, nearly three times as high.

The girls watched as she began to climb steadily upward as if she had memorized every hand and foothold in the rock. When she was about five feet above their heads, she looked back. "Well, what are you standing there for?" she scolded. "Start climbing."

Another wave, the most powerful one yet, was all the incentive they needed to begin pulling themselves up the rock wall behind Mrs. Fitzlagen. Molly reached up and started to climb. She found that she couldn't move as quickly as the nimble little woman. She had to search slowly and carefully for each new nook in which to place her hands and feet but, slowly, she began to ascend. Ashley was right behind her.

"Come on. Come on," Mrs. Fitzlagen urged. "The tide rises quickly."

Before very long, they were almost twelve feet above the water. Glancing back, Molly saw that the water was nearly four feet deep and still coming in fast. When she looked back—Mrs. Fitzlagen was gone.

"Where'd she go?" she asked, looking at Ashley.

"I couldn't tell. I was looking back at that last wave."

"Me, too." They kept climbing until they were nearly to the ceiling. Only then did they see the dim light of a cloudy day. Reaching forward, Molly touched cold, smooth rock. A hand firmly clasped her wrist and pulled her forward.

The hand belonged to Mrs. Fitzlagen, who had climbed out first and waited for them aboveground. Daylight—even grim, cloudy daylight—had never been so wonderfully welcome before. Molly breathed deeply, drinking in the salt air, elated to be free of the dark, flooding cavern below.

She turned and reached into the hole just as Ashley's hands surfaced. "We made it!" Molly shouted triumphantly as she pulled Ashley up through the opening.

The moment Ashley was out and sitting, she began to quiver and cry. Mrs. Fitzlagen patted her shoulder soothingly. "There, there, child. It was frightening, but you're safe now."

Ashley wiped her eyes. "Yes. Thank you. Thank you," she whispered.

They were on a wide shelf of rock halfway up one of the towering cliffs, overlooking the crashing, wind-tossed ocean. "Where were we?" Molly asked Mrs. Fitzlagen.

"You were in a cave," the woman said simply.

"We know, but how did you know about it?" Ashley asked.

With rough vigor, Mrs. Fitzlagen brushed water from her wet hair. "I've been around these parts for longer than you can imagine. There's not an inch of them I don't know."

"Who left all those things down there?" Molly asked.

"Different children have played in that cave at different times. I haven't seen a child about the place for some time, though. I believe the last one in there was a little boy, adorable he was, too. He left these parts, though. Haven't seen him in many years. He's a grown man now, I assume."

"But the lantern. It was still burning," Molly pointed out.

Mrs. Fitzlagen shrugged philosophically. "Indeed it was."

Ashley pulled off one sneaker and poured water from it. "We'd better find Katie and Christina and let them know we're all right," she said. "They must be so worried."

The climb down to the beach was unbelievably easy. Just as they were about to set foot on the beach, Molly saw Christina and Katie racing breathlessly toward them. "What happened? How did you get up there?" Katie asked in a rush of words.

"Mrs. Fitzlagen saved us," Molly told them solemnly.

Together, Christina and Katie wrapped their arms around Ashley and Molly. "I was so scared," Katie said, choking back a sob. "I didn't know what to do."

Christina just held on tight as tears streamed down her cheeks.

Until she felt the warmth of their embraces, Molly hadn't realized how cold she'd been. She'd probably been too scared about the most immediate danger— drowning—to even be aware of it.

"Come girls," said Mrs. Fitzlagen. "My cottage is not far. You need to warm up and dry off. The two of you are positively blue and I can see your friends have had a time of it, too. That drafty old castle isn't the best place to get warm and, anyway, it's too far. Follow me."

With chattering teeth, Molly went along with the others as Mrs. Fitzlagen led them up a winding path, off the beach. The walk was an easy one and soon Molly spied a low, stone cabin with a thatched roof.

"It sure looks like a leprechaun's house," Ashley whispered to her, coming up from behind.

"I know," Molly agreed, nodding. "It does."

They followed Mrs. Fitzlagen in. The cottage was warm and cozy with heavy beams across the ceiling and a stone hearth aglow with a small, steady fire. The ceiling was so low that Katie and Christina could easily have reached up and touched the rough wooden beams.

"Now, who'd like some tea?" Mrs. Fitzlagen said briskly, turning a knob on the small white stove and igniting a friendly blue flame beneath a large black kettle.

The girls heartily agreed that all of them would. Mrs. Fitzlagen filled a brown teapot with a handful of loose tea, then pulled two plaid blankets from a polished wooden chest by the fireplace. "Why not take off those wet things and let them dry by the fire," she said to Molly and Ashley. "You can wrap yourselves in these."

"Thanks," Molly said, taking the blanket.

Christina and Katie warmed themselves by the fire, the soaked legs of their jeans drying as they stood. Molly and Ashley wrapped themselves in the soft blankets and began pulling off their drenched clothing.

As Molly unzipped her jeans, something poked her back. The odd book she'd found in the cave, the one she'd stuck in the waistband of her pants, tumbled to the floor.

Amazingly dry, it flipped open. It seemed to be a sketchbook of some kind. Molly bent to retrieve it. As she picked it up, her breath caught in her throat.

"What?" Christina asked. "What's wrong?"

Molly held the sketchbook in her hands. "This drawing," she murmured, unable to take her eyes from the soft-colored pastel. "It's a picture of me."

10

That night, after dinner, Molly stayed alone in the large bedroom. She lay across the canopied bed and stared down at the drawing in the sketchbook. The woman looked *so* much like Molly, she was almost a twin. Except now that Molly really studied it, she could see this was an older woman with a rounder, fuller face. Molly could see, too, that *this* woman was pretty, much prettier than Molly. And yet, they looked alike. How could that be?

The woman stared back at her, smiling with large, bright eyes beneath wispy blonde bangs. Her hair was swept back in a loose twist. Stray tendrils framed her happy face. Her cobalt blue dress was wide at the shoulders. Molly guessed she wore shoulder pads. From the look of her double's outfit, Molly guessed the sketch had been made a long time ago—maybe in the 1940s.

She slid from the bed and crossed to an ornate oval mirror hung between the two long windows facing the courtyard. Staring at her own face, Molly held the sketch up next to her cheek.

For more than five minutes she stood like that, her eyes darting back and forth, examining and comparing the two faces, her own and the sketch Mrs. Fitzlagen had immediately identified as her grandmother's. Molly's mind was blank. She was simply looking. Looking.

After a few more minutes, she slowly began to chew her lower lip. There was no denying it. Compared to the face in the sketchbook, Molly looked sick. Her neck appeared scrawny. Her cheekbones were too sharp. The hollows of her cheeks seemed sunken, almost skeletal. Even her eyes had a wide, haunted, oddly familiar look. She'd seen that look somewhere else.

Where? Molly wondered. Then she realized where. She'd seen the same look in the eyes of starving children in impoverished, war-torn countries, children she'd seen on TV or in magazine photos.

Thinking of magazines brought another realization. In a way, an even more frightening one. She'd sometimes seen the same look in the eyes of certain fashion models—the same unnaturally wide-open, hungry look.

Molly lowered the sketch and turned from the mirror. Her mind whirled. Did she look like a starving child or like a glamorous fashion model? Or did the fashion model look like a starving child? And if she did, why was she so admired?

Ashley came into the room dressed in her plaid nightgown. "Are you all right?" she asked. "You look terrible."

"What do you mean?" Molly asked sharply.

"I mean you look upset," Ashley faltered. "That's all. You had a funny look when I came in, like something was wrong."

"Oh," Molly said, relieved. "I thought you meant my looks looked terrible."

"No," Ashley said softly, coming up beside Molly. "What's the matter?" She noticed the book in Molly's hand. "Isn't that the sketchbook we found?"

Molly nodded and handed it to her. "Wow!" Ashley gasped. "You really *do* look like her," she said, looking down at the sketch.

"Mrs. Fitzlagen said the same thing," Molly told her. "Do you think I'll look like this when I get older?"

"Probably," Ashley said, picking up the sketch and studying it. "If you gain some weight."

"If I was thinner I would have gotten through that tunnel easily. I wouldn't have gotten wedged there like I did," Molly said, somehow still searching for a valid, reasonable need to be thin.

Ashley's green eyes narrowed. "That's pretty crazy. How often are you going to be squeezing through rock tunnels? It's not like that happens every day. I mean, you'll want to fit between the cracks in the sidewalk next."

"I know . . . maybe I am too thin. I mean, maybe . . . but I don't want to be fat," Molly trailed off miserably.

"Your grandmother isn't *fat*. She just weighs more. Look at her in this picture. She looks fine."

"People were fatter back then. Nobody cared. Things are different now," Molly said.

"Not that different. You don't want to land back in the hospital, do you?" Ashley asked, concerned. "I thought you were feeling so much better about yourself and your weight since . . . since you know, you met the angel. Aren't you still feeling that way?"

"I was for awhile," Ashley confessed, turning away. "But if the angel loved me so much . . . ." Molly turned her head away, embarrassed by the tears that sprang unexpectedly to her eyes.

"What?" Ashley prompted gently.

"Then where is she?" Molly asked, whisking away a tear. "What good is someone's love if they're not there to prove it every day? Isn't it all just words?"

"I don't know," Ashley answered quietly, resting her hand softly on Molly's shoulder.

Molly wasn't sure what had put her into this sad mood. Maybe she was more upset about almost being trapped in the cave than she'd realized. Or perhaps it was later, returning to the castle with no one but old Mrs. Loughlin there to greet them. It might have been the sketch. Or maybe it was all the phone calls during dinner.

The phone in the dining room—the only room with a phone——rang continually while they ate the nourishing lamb stew Mrs. Loughlin had made. Alice called Christina from her hotel room. She reported that Lucky Feather had come in first at the racetrack that day. Then Katie got a long-distance call from Aunt Rainie and Uncle Jeff. After that, Mr. and Mrs. Kingsley called. Ashley poured out the story of their being trapped in the cave. "No, don't be upset. I'm fine now. Really," she told them. It took her a five full minutes to calm them down. Molly could hear the phone squawking their concern and worry while Ashley soothed them.

Molly sat at the long table eating her stew and listening to all these loving conversations. And waiting for the phone to ring—for *her* call. In her head, she practiced telling the story of being trapped in the cave so that it wouldn't sound too frightening. She didn't want her parents, whichever one called first, to be too angry with her. Yet she didn't want to make it sound as if it hadn't been *any* big deal. She wanted them to be alarmed enough to give her *some* sympathy. By the end of dinner, she knew exactly how she would tell it.

But the call never came.

She'd gone to her room and taken her cellular phone from her luggage. She'd phoned her mother, but only reached the answering machine. "It's me, Molly," she'd left a message. "I'm . . . fine. Bye."

That was probably it, Molly decided, turning back to face Ashley.

That was when the blue mood had set in.

"I think you should get to sleep," Ashley said. "I'm really tired and all scraped up from climbing. You must be, too."

"Where are Christina and Katie?"

"Christina is downstairs in the library reading a book about leprechauns. And Katie's in the main room with Mrs. Loughlin. She's telling Katie stories about old Ireland or something like that, and Katie's writing them down. It's for her story she's working on."

Molly shut the sketchbook. "Katie's lucky to have her writing. Do you know what you want to do when you're older?"

"Something with horses, I guess," Ashley said, walking around the bed and climbing in the other side. "My grandparents owned the ranch before us, and I've always lived around horses. I *like* horses, so I suppose that's what I'll do."

"You're lucky, too, then," Molly said as she reached to turn off the lamp on the night table. "I want to do something I'll probably never get to do."

"Be an astronaut?" Ashley asked in the dark.

"Yeah," Molly said as she plumped her pillow. "My parents think it's crazy. They don't think I can do it."

"Do you think you can?" Ashley asked in a sleepy voice.

"I don't know," Molly admitted. It hadn't occurred to her to try to become an astronaut without her parents' express approval. How could she possibly do *anything* without it?

* * *

The next morning, Molly's eyes snapped open abruptly. Loud, excited voices rose up from the courtyard below the window.

Ashley bolted up beside her. "What's going on out there?" she asked, tossing off her covers.

The shouts and laughter grew louder. Katie pulled a pillow over her head to block out the commotion, but Christina was already up and standing by the window in her white flannel nightgown. "They've brought Lucky Feather back!" she announced excitedly.

"Lucky Feather!" Molly cried, leaping from the bed. "I thought they were keeping him in Connemare." Rushing to the window, she looked down at the gleaming, regal black stallion galloping in a circle with Alice on his back. Mr. and Mrs. Kingsley stood nearby, watching. Mr.

Morgan folded his arms and studied Lucky Feather intently.

Molly grabbed jeans and a sweatshirt and quickly dressed. "Wait for us," Ashley called as Molly hurried out the door, her long hair flying loosely around her shoulders like a pale blonde cloud.

"I'll meet you down there," Molly called back to her. She ran down the twisting hallways, down the wide stone steps, through the dining room, and out the back room to the courtyard.

Mrs. Kingsley spotted her first and smiled. "He's a beauty, isn't he? You should have seen him run yesterday. He flew."

Molly shielded her eyes from the morning sun and studied the glistening stallion. He *was* a beauty. Majestic. Proud and strong. Alone of all the horses she'd ever known, his proportions were completely perfect. Lucky Feather's magnificence tugged at Molly's heart. She couldn't remember ever feeling this moved before, certainly not by a horse.

"He's a purebred Irish champion," Mr. Morgan said proudly, striding toward them.

Alice brought Lucky Feather to a halt in front of Molly. Gingerly, Molly ran her hand along his glossy coat. "He's gorgeous," she sighed.

Something about the horse was truly inspiring to her. He awed her and made her heartbeat quicken. It had to be his beauty—his astounding, perfect beauty. Yet there was more. The horse's black eyes bored into hers, and Molly felt a tingle of unspoken communication dart between them.

Molly couldn't take her eyes off Lucky Feather. It was as if the horse's life force was so powerful, so vital, it created a field of energy around him. Standing within that field made Molly feel at once warm and peaceful, yet brimming with energy as if some of the force were actually touching her, like an electric charge.

Did everyone feel this? she wondered. Molly looked around. No. No one else appeared to be reacting in any way out of the ordinary. Only her father was paying attention. He stood, watching her interact with the horse. She smiled at him and he smiled back, a brief sparkling smile like the sun suddenly coming through on a cloudy day. "Can I ride him, Dad?" Molly asked impulsively.

Mr. Morgan's brows furrowed in incredulous disbelief. "I should say not! This is a champion racehorse. It's not a toy."

"But you know I can ride," Molly insisted.

Mr. Morgan waved her away dismissively. "Molly, please. I can't afford to have this horse mishandled. It's too large an investment."

With a soft nicker, Lucky Feather took several steps away from her. This, combined with her father's abrupt refusal, soured Molly's mood. Her feeling of calm joy was shattered.

"*He's* too large an investment," Molly corrected her father sullenly, annoyed at the way her father referred to this amazing creature as *it*. "He's not an it."

"Molly, don't act the spoiled brat, please," Mr. Morgan snapped. "I don't have the time for it right now."

He turned his back on Molly and began talking to Mr. Kingsley in a low, businesslike voice.

Cut to the quick by his sharp words, Molly stood there, staring at his broad back. A deep red flush crept up her face as an angry sob formed in her throat. She fought it down until only a petulant huff came out her mouth. Mr. Morgan didn't notice. He wasn't even paying attention to her anymore. She might as well have vanished, for all he knew.

Molly's cheeks burned as if her father's rejecting words had hit her like an actual, physical slap. She bit her lip to fight down tears.

Was she being a spoiled brat, asking to ride—pushing the issue, even?

No. She wasn't. It wasn't only being dismissed as a brat that hurt her feelings. It was that her father didn't think she could do it. Wouldn't even consider the possibility that she could, even though he *knew* she could ride and jump. He, of all people, he who had paid for her *dressage* lessons at the club all these years—he should know she could handle a horse. Of course, if he'd ever *once* shown up at one of her competitions, maybe he'd be more sure of it. Still, he didn't have to belittle her skill with horses.

And why did he have to talk to her like that, so rudely, as if her feelings didn't matter, like she was some sort of pest? He made her feel so small—and in front of everyone, too!

Molly caught Alice's eye. Alice seemed to be studying her with pity in her eyes. Embarrassed, Molly smiled. "Why didn't you take him to the farm in Connemare?" she asked.

"I don't know," Alice replied, tucking a strand of hair

behind her ear. "Your father just changed his mind and decided he'd prefer him to stay here. There *is* an old stable down on the other side of this courtyard. The roof is down in one spot, but it can be boarded over and made usable."

"Cool," Molly said. "I'm glad he's here."

Alice nodded and sighed. "He's awfully beautiful. And fast!"

Mr. Kingsley took Lucky Feather and hitched him to the stone fence. "Let's go see what that stable really needs," he suggested to the other adults. They walked off down a path that cut through the bare woods. Molly was alone with Lucky Feather.

The horse whinnied softly and swiveled his head back to gaze at Molly with deep, piercing eyes. She stared at him, once again mesmerized, her strong connection to this animal returning. His gaze seemed to look deep into her heart. Stroking his neck, she laid her cheek against his side.

Molly had never experienced anything like this. She struggled to define the feeling and the word *ancient* drifted to mind. That was it. There was something very old about her connection to this horse. She shut her eyes and saw a picture. It was herself dressed as a medieval princess, sheer fabrics fluttering around her heavy brocade dress. She rode a magnificent black horse. Was it really Molly? Was the horse Lucky Feather?

Opening her eyes, she stared hard at Lucky Feather. Had that picture been a flight of imagination or some sort of memory? She'd never know and it really didn't matter.

Stroking the black forelock between his high, pointed ears, Molly longed to ride him, to feel the wind whip past them as they galloped over the fields. Not being able to brought back that old feeling of always standing on the outside, watching—not really being involved in life.

Everyone was down at the stable. They'd be busy down there for awhile. Who would ever know if she rode Lucky Feather right now?

With a quick glance down the path, Molly unhitched Lucky Feather. He was so tall she found it a little difficult to pull herself up into the saddle. But once she did, a new sense of strength and wild freedom immediately coursed through her. Clicking softly, Molly squeezed her knees into his sides to get him moving. He cantered smoothly at first. Then Molly leaned forward and let out the reins.

As if a tremendous wind had swept them up, Lucky Feather raced swiftly and smoothly around the courtyard. Handling him was almost effortless. He moved as if one with the wind.

Molly had never before felt so completely at ease in the saddle. She might have been one with the horse as they moved together in a soaring, fluid motion.

From the corner of her eye she saw Ashley, Katie, and Christina sitting on the stone fence watching her. She thought they were looking very impressed. Molly felt proud and leaned further forward in the saddle, digging her heels into Lucky Feather's smooth, muscular side, urging him to go faster.

Was she showing off? Who cared? She felt wonderful. Lucky Feather heeded her silent command and ran even faster. He, too, seemed to exult in the pace and freedom of running. Molly imagined he was a winged Pegasus about to soar into the air. If he really had, she'd hardly have been surprised.

Molly had learned to jump a horse. Could Lucky Feather jump? Probably. This horse could do anything. Maybe he couldn't really leap into the sky. Certainly, though, he could jump that two-foot high bench in the center of the courtyard. Molly had to find out how it would feel. It *had* to feel like flying.

Steering him with the reins, she rode Lucky Feather to the farthest corner of the courtyard before turning him toward the bench in the center. She waved quickly to her friends and then began racing toward the bench.

Molly raised herself in the saddle, getting into position to jump. They were nearly there, not more than a few yards from the bench when a sudden sound made her look up.

"Molly!" her father bellowed, his face purple with rage. "Molly!" He stood at the entrance to the path, his fists balled at his sides in fury.

Seized with panic, Molly pulled up tightly on the reins.

Lucky Feather's shrill, angry trumpeting split the air as he reared back and the leather reins ripped from Molly's hands.

11

"Molly!"

Molly opened her eyes and stared up at the sky from where she lay sprawled on her back on the stony ground. Lucky Feather had run off, she couldn't tell where.

"Molly! Molly! Are you all right?" Her friends' voices grew louder as they raced to help her. Soon they were gathered around, looking down at her with frantic, worried expressions. Ashley, Katie, and Christina.

Where was her father?

"Are you all right? Can you move?" Katie asked, kneeling down beside her.

Molly opened her mouth to reply, but no sound came out. Her fall had knocked the wind out of her. She propped herself up on her elbows and the ground under her pitched violently. A wave of nausea swept over her. She lay down again.

"She doesn't look so good," Ashley said, concerned. "Lie flat, Molly. Your dad went after Lucky Feather. He'll be here in a minute."

"He's not having much luck," Christina observed, looking across the field to where Mr. Morgan chased the nervously prancing Lucky Feather. "I'd better go help him."

Dad went after Lucky Feather, Molly thought bitterly. *That figured. Lucky Feather is an important investment. I'm just his worthless daughter.*

Hot pain flashed across her forehead. It spread along her cheekbones and down through her jaw. It occurred to her in a horrifying rush of worry that maybe she'd really hurt herself. Panicked, she tried to move her foot.

It moved.

She was able to bend her arms and her legs, too.

Again, she tried to sit up. The pain in her head increased, forcing her to squeeze her eyes shut to control it. When she opened them again, her father stood before her.

"Do you think anything is broken?" he asked softly, squatting down beside her.

Molly shook her head, still unable to speak. He reached out to her. "Come on now. Try to get up. I'll help you, Molly. It's okay."

She took his hand and let him pull her up. As she stood, she took in big gulps of air. The effort made her chest hurt. Her head ached. Hiccups wracked her thin frame as the air reentered her lungs. Tears rolled down her cheeks.

"What's wrong?" her father asked. "Tell me where it hurts."

"My head," she managed to say. "It aches horribly. I'm . . . I'm dizzy. I feel sick, too. My stomach."

"Maybe she has a concussion," Katie suggested.

"Come inside," her father said, putting his arm around her. "Get into bed and rest today. I'll have Mrs. Loughlin keep an eye on you while you sleep. If you still feel bad tomorrow, we'll find you a doctor."

Molly let her father help her walk to the castle. Glancing to the side, she saw Christina hitching Lucky Feather to the fence. The horse looked at her with what seemed a sympathetic expression. It wasn't his fault she had fallen. She'd yanked his reins so hard when her father yelled that it must have hurt and shocked him, especially happening when it did, just as he was preparing to jump.

He looked so noble there, tethered to the fence, like a prince in exile. The further Molly got from him, the weaker, more achy she felt. She glanced at him one last time before entering the castle, feeling as if she couldn't stand to have him out of her sight.

By the time Molly reached her bedroom, her head felt as if it was about to explode. Mrs. Loughlin bustled in and took over, helping Molly undress and get into bed.

Soon Molly fell asleep. When she awoke, the room was empty. Flickering shadows danced along the wall from the fire burning in the grate. The searing pain in her head had subsided to a dull, steady ache, but her stomach still felt queasy. The door creaked open and her father looked in. "I'm awake," she said weakly, still groggy from her sleep.

He came and stood beside her bed. "What possessed you, Molly?" he asked in a neutral voice. "You could have seriously damaged that horse. You know what would have happened if he'd broken his leg jumping."

Molly did know and the idea made her shudder. A broken leg never mended properly. More than likely, Lucky Feather would have been put down, killed, if he'd broken his leg. For certain, his days as a racehorse would end.

"I'm sorry," Molly said sincerely, tears filling her eyes at the thought that she could have injured Lucky Feather. But then another thought came to her. Lucky Feather wouldn't have broken his leg. Molly knew how to jump. It was only her father who was making her feel as if she might have hurt him. That Molly herself might have been hurt didn't seem to matter to him at all.

" 'Sorry' hardly covers it," Mr. Morgan insisted, unforgiving. "You knew my wishes, yet you deliberately disobeyed me. I don't understand it. Really, I do not."

"I thought I could ride him," Molly said in a low, sullen tone. "I could, too. Everything would have been all right if you hadn't come along and shouted."

"Oh, this is my fault, is it?" Mr. Morgan scoffed disdainfully.

"No, but . . . in a way," Molly trailed off hopelessly. She could never explain, not to him.

"Molly, you didn't know for certain if you could ride him or even if he could jump."

"Can't he?" Molly asked in a small voice.

"Yes, he's a champion jumper, but that is not the point. The point is that he does not belong to you and you violated my wishes. By the way, how are you feeling?" Mr. Morgan added.

Molly shot him a hurt glance. Shouldn't that question have come at the beginning of this conversation? "I feel awful," she told him bluntly.

"What hurts?"

Was Molly imagining it or did he seem worried? "Everything."

"Well, I suppose that's to be expected after the fall you took," her father said calmly.

Molly felt a sudden, violent urge to jump up and pound on his chest. Why was he so stiff, so cold? Why did he have to be that way? What was so wrong with her that he couldn't love her? If he loved her, he'd be frantic with worry right now. He wouldn't come in just to scold her about riding Lucky Feather.

She glared at him and the force of her own anger frightened her. How *could* she be so angry at him—he was her father! She loved him.

His eyes widened, surprised by the fierce look on her face. He took a step back and folded his arms.

A deep panic took hold of Molly. What had she done? With one look she'd pushed him even further away. That was the last thing she wanted. The very last thing!

"Dad, I'm sorry. I don't know why I did it. Please don't be angry with me. Please. I feel so awful." As she spoke, her mind raced. Did she mean these things or did she just want to win him over? She honestly didn't know.

It worked, though. He unfolded his arms and sat on the edge of her bed. "Go back to sleep," he said kindly. "You look pale."

Heartened by the concern in his voice, Molly wanted to keep him there. "I found my grandmother's grave the other day," she told him.

"Yes, it's down on the slope below the castle, I believe," he said, looking away.

"What was she like?" Molly asked.

"She died when I was so young, I barely remember," her father said quickly.

"How old were you?" Molly wanted to know.

"Eleven."

"And you don't remember?" she persisted. It seemed that at eleven he should have remembered something about her. She'd been eleven herself not long ago and she could remember everything.

"No. It was a long time ago," he said, turning toward the window.

He's lying, said a small voice inside her. What told her that? Was it the uncomfortable look on his face, the way his eyes shifted away, or was it the slightly shaky timber of his usually firm, unshakable voice? She couldn't be sure, but she was certain he wasn't being truthful.

Besides, an eleven-year-old might forget some things, but surely not his parents.

Thinking of her grandmother reminded her of the lost watch. Molly hid her right wrist under the covers. She didn't want him to notice she wasn't wearing it. Not that he would. He didn't usually notice much about what she wore.

"Why is your mother buried here if you lived in England?" Molly asked.

"This was her home. She loved it more than anything. And, she died here."

"She did? I don't understand."

"When she grew ill, she wanted to live here. Perhaps she wanted to die here. I don't know. But we were here when she died. As I said, it was long ago and it's all very vague to me now." He stood, signaling that the conversation was over.

Molly nodded, losing the energy to ask more questions. The pain in her head was growing again. "Could you get me an aspirin?" she asked pleadingly.

"I'll send Mrs. Loughlin in with something," he said. "Now, get some rest." He turned to leave and then turned back. "By the way, Molly, I noticed you haven't been wearing your silver watch lately. Is it broken?"

Stunned by this unexpected observation, Molly paled and pulled her arm closer to her side beneath the comforter. "No, I . . ." Her voice caught in her suddenly dry throat. How could she tell him she'd lost it?

But . . . but maybe she could. He was being kind to her. And even speaking about his mother a little. When he talked about her, he seemed different somehow. Younger. Less forbidding. She didn't want to lie to him now.

"I lost it," she admitted sadly.

"Molly!" he cried, his face darkening.

"I took it off the other day in the graveyard and—"

"Molly, that watch is irreplaceable."

"I know. I went back for it but . . ." she trailed off miserably as her father thundered over her.

"And you were talking about training to be an astronaut! Can you imagine?" he said with a mirthless laugh. "You ask me for things, Molly, but you can't even take care of the things you already have. You want to go to Space Camp, but how can you expect to be an astronaut when you can't even be responsible for keeping track of a small watch? Do you see how irresponsible it was to lose the watch?"

What was she supposed to say? Yes, I do see? No, and I hate you for making me feel so small? She couldn't say either one. Either answer would have made her feel even worse. There was nothing *to* say, so she swallowed hard. It felt like she was swallowing a bitter drink.

"I'll go ask Mrs. Loughlin for that medicine," her father said as he left the room.

Molly turned to her side away from him and silently wet her pillow with her tears.

12

"You've *got* to eat something," Christina insisted. "You were doing so well, you don't want to start slipping back now." They were the last two left at the long table that morning. The adults and Ashley had gone down to the stable. Katie had gone outside with her notebook in hand.

Molly looked at the scrambled eggs on her plate. They looked rubbery and they smelled awful. She couldn't bring herself to eat them or any of the usual huge breakfast that had been laid out that morning. Her appetite had completely vanished.

"Do you think it was your fall? Are you still feeling bad?" Christina asked.

"Maybe. My head is a little achy right on top. My stomach is kind of rocky, too."

"Did you tell your father?" Christina wanted to know.

Molly shrugged. "What for? He's busy." There was no way she was going to tell him she didn't feel well. He didn't care. He probably just came in to check on her last night because he thought he should. Not because he really cared. It was just his *fatherly duty*. Yes, that was how Commander Demander would see it. It was his duty to check on her health, just part of his job.

"I'll tell him for you," Christina volunteered eagerly.

Molly reached across the table and clutched her wrist. "Don't. Please. He's mad enough at me for riding Lucky Feather. I don't want to remind him of it by dragging this thing out."

"What do you mean?"

"If he has to take me to a doctor, he'll be remembering why the whole time. I want him to just forget it, for it to be over with." For a moment, Molly stopped and imagined a different father, one who doted on her, adored her. He'd have sat up all night with her, watching while she slept to be sure she was all right. He wouldn't have gone out today. He'd have had a doctor come just to make sure she was all right.

But that wasn't her father. Not Commander Demander. He probably thought she deserved to feel bad as punishment for disobeying his royal command. And now that he knew she'd lost his mother's watch, she was less than nothing in his eyes. No. She wasn't going to bother him over a headache and a stomachache. Not likely.

"What if you have a concussion?" Christina pressed.

"A girl in my riding class had a concussion last year. The doctor just sent her home and told her to take it easy," Molly recalled, getting up from her chair.

"A doctor is supposed to check you, though," Christina protested, "to make sure there's nothing worse wrong with you."

"There isn't," Molly said confidently. "I'll take it easy today, all right?"

Christina studied her, looking worried. "All right," she said reluctantly as she stood up. "I should go down to the stable and help out. That's the reason I'm here, after all. You should go back to bed."

"I'm not sleepy, but I'll hang out and read or do something quiet like that," Molly assured her, smiling. "Okay?"

Christina nodded and left the dining room. As soon as she was gone, Molly dropped her face into her hands. She hadn't wanted Christina to know how bad she really felt. Her head still ached ferociously and her stomach lurched whenever she moved. Her vision was off, too. Everything had a fuzzy edge to it. If she concentrated, she could sharpen her focus, but it was too tiring to do it constantly.

Molly didn't want to make a big deal about it, though. As she'd told Christina, she didn't want to do anything to remind her father of the reason she felt bad. And she certainly didn't want to land back in a hospital. She'd seen enough of hospitals to last the rest of her life. Besides, she didn't want everyone making a fuss over her—not for being ill. She'd had enough of that, too. It made her feel like everyone in the world was stronger and more able to cope with things than she was. It made her feel weak and helpless, and she hated feeling that way.

Drawing in a deep, steadying breath, Molly stood again and walked down the stairs, through the small back room, and out to the courtyard. At the far corner of the stone fence Katie stood, looking out at the ocean. Molly crossed the yard. As she neared Katie, Molly saw that she was taking pictures. Her trusty black-and-white notebook lay open on top of the stone fence.

"What are you doing?" Molly asked, coming up alongside her.

Katie jumped at the sound of her voice. "Oh, wow," she said, laughing. "You startled me. I want to take pictures of this place so I'll never forget it. I don't see how I could, but you never know. I want the pictures for my story, too."

"What are you writing?" Molly leaned up against the fence and gazed out over the wild ocean.

Katie looked away uneasily, then turned back. "I hope you don't mind. I'm writing about your grandmother," she confided.

"My grandmother?" Molly was a little surprised.

"Mrs. Loughlin told me some things about her the other night, and I thought they'd make a cool story."

"What kinds of things?" Molly wanted to know.

"Well, like that her parents forbade her to marry your grandfather because he wasn't Irish and he didn't have a lot of money. He was in the British navy during World War II. But your grandmother married him anyway, so her parents told her never to come back."

"How mean!" Molly said. "That's horrible."

"I know. And this castle was her home. She would never be able to see it again. But when her parents died, they left the castle to her, and the first thing she did was come right back. Mrs. Loughlin said she loved this castle so much."

"I suppose that's why she wanted to be buried here," Molly reasoned. "You know what's strange? Her parents really loved her enough to leave the castle to her, but they couldn't let her know that while they were still alive. That is *so* sad."

"That's the theme of my story," Katie said, her eyes alight with enthusiasm. "You got it right away. I've been thinking about my own parents, you know. They always let me know they loved me. You know, with hugs and kisses and talking to me and stuff like that. And even though they're . . . gone . . . I know they love me and they'll always take care of me." Katie fell silent a moment, her face unreadable. "I mean," she went on carefully, "they left that money so I could come here on this trip and go to college and everything. It's like they're still looking after me, in a way. I guess I was luckier than I knew."

"You *are* lucky," Molly agreed in a low, unhappy voice. Odd, she thought. She had more than a name in common with her grandmother. They both had parents who were cold. Did Molly's parents really love her? she wondered. Maybe they didn't. Maybe they had her because having a child was what they thought they should do. More *duty*. Sure, they gave her stuff. Stuff was great. But it wasn't love.

"You don't look so hot," Katie observed.

"I'm okay," Molly insisted. "I thought I'd go look for my watch again. I've got to find it. I just have to. I'm going to cover every inch of that graveyard until I do. Do you want to come?"

"If you don't mind, I'd like to stay here and work on this," Katie said. "Anyway, shouldn't you rest?"

"I can't rest until I find my watch," Molly said, pulling herself on to the fence and swinging her legs over. "I'm going to check the graveyard, anyway."

Molly found the narrow dirt path that led to the graveyard and followed it through the thorny branches and bare trees until she came to the small patch of graves and monuments. The walk tired her more quickly than it should have. Despite the cold wind, she was wet with perspiration.

Weaving her way through the stones, Molly reached the angel monument. She gazed down at her own name, Molly Morgan, etched at the angel's bare foot. Who was this woman? she wondered. Molly wished she'd known her. Molly thought she'd have liked her. It seemed she had a lot of spirit.

With a sigh, Molly began methodically searching for her silver watch. It had to be somewhere nearby. She stopped a moment to inspect the repaired crack in the angel's wing. It was unbelievable. Mrs. Fitzlagen had done an amazing job. Like a healed wound, the wing revealed only the finest line where the crack had been.

Molly ran her fingers gingerly along the trace of the crack. Suddenly, unexpectedly, she started to cry. Like a sudden storm, the sobs racked her delicate frame. "Why can't he love me?" The words burst from her lips as she stood, clutching the angel's wing. Trying to believe that maybe he really did—in his own silent way, deep, deep inside—wasn't enough anymore. She needed to see it, to feel it. "Why can't he show me?" she cried, pressing her forehead into the cool stone wing. Her inner hurt was so strong it made her heart ache. "If I could just see some sign that he loved me, I wouldn't feel so bad all the time. I wouldn't hate myself."

She suddenly realized that she was talking to the statue as if it were a real angel. "Please give me some sign," she whispered into the stone. "Please."

Molly stayed that way, her forehead and hand on the wing, for several minutes until her tears subsided. Wiping her eyes, she looked up and sniffed. Crying wasn't going to do her any good. She had to find that watch. Maybe that would win her father's respect, at least.

With a last sniffle, she walked around the wing, intent on resuming her search. As she reached the back of the angel, she stopped short. Mrs. Fitzlagen lay between the wings, curled up and snoring gently. Her bowl of cement and a wide trowel lay on the ground beside her.

Her green eyes fluttered open. Molly's soft, startled gasp must have awakened her. "Well, hello, dear," she said, sitting up. "I must have dozed off. I was putting the final touches on that angel wing. It was so hard hanging onto the wing with one hand and working with the other, without you and your friend here to help me like the other day. When I sat down to rest I must have fallen asleep. Silly me."

"You did a wonderful job," Molly said sincerely.

Mrs. Fitzlagen stood, her head just about level with Molly's shoulder. She dusted the dry grass from her green pants. "That's what I do," she said matter-of-factly. "I fix broken wings. I've been doing it for so many years I should be good at it by now."

"Only wings?" Molly asked.

"No," Mrs. Fitzlagen replied. "Sometimes heads break and need repair. The neck is often a weak point because the stone gets narrow there." She stopped and studied Molly.

Molly realized her face must be tearstained and puffy. She turned away self-consciously. She knew how blotchy crying made her. It must be so obvious to Mrs. Fitzlagen.

"Hearts often crack, too," Mrs. Fitzlagen said softly. "It's difficult to see those, though. It's hard to fix what you can't see."

"Hearts?" Molly asked, checking the other monuments for hearts. She didn't see any. Was Mrs. Fitzlagen talking about her, Molly? Was she talking about Molly's heart?

Mrs. Fitzlagen began putting her cementing tools back into her bag. "Of course. Hearts break the easiest of all. They simply crack and fall apart. They're not good for much after that. They're the hardest to repair, too."

"How can you repair the heart of a statue?" Molly asked. "A statue doesn't have a heart."

"How do you know?" Mrs. Fitzlagen asked.

"Because, well . . . they're stone."

"Some *people* seem like stone, too, don't they," Mrs. Fitzlagen said. "It's a sad thing, possibly the saddest thing in the world."

Molly felt weak and sat on the ground. She didn't know what Mrs. Fitzlagen was talking about, but she didn't feel strong enough to figure it out.

"You don't look so good, my girl," Mrs. Fitzlagen said kindly.

Molly told her what had happened. She just let

everything pour out of her, how she'd ridden Lucky Feather and been thrown. Without knowing exactly why, she went on to tell how her father had been angry and how bad he made her feel. "I suppose I wish he were worried sick about me instead of angry," she admitted. "Shouldn't a father feel that way about his daughter?"

Mrs. Fitzlagen nodded sympathetically. "Your father sounds like his very own father."

"He does?"

"Aye. Your grandfather never could show his emotions. It was like he was afraid of them. He made himself hard when he wasn't really hard at all."

"Was he mean to my grandmother?" Molly asked.

Mrs. Fitzlagen smiled softly. "No. Your grandmother was the only one who saw his soft side. Maybe it was because she had the gift of looking deep and not just seeing what was on the surface. But after she died . . . after that, he had one of those broken hearts that just wouldn't be mended. Maybe your father has one of those cracked hearts, too."

"My father?" Molly asked. "Why would you say that?"

Mrs. Fitzlagen patted Molly's shoulder. "I suppose to answer that, you'd have to have the gift like your dear grandmother had, the gift of looking deep."

Molly couldn't imagine her father having a broken heart. He was so strong and in control. She didn't know about anything in his life that was heartbreaking. Mrs. Fitzlagen must be mistaken.

"Have you seen my silver watch?" she asked, feeling uncomfortable with the conversation, wanting to change it. "I put it in the bowl when we were working on the wing the other day and when I went back for it, it was gone. It was my grandmother's and my father is really furious at me for losing it. I've just got to find it."

"Sometimes you have to lose things before you're able to really find them," Mrs. Fitzlagen commented cryptically.

What was she talking about? Molly wondered. "Sure. I mean, of course," she said. "You can't find something if it's not lost."

"Precisely," Mrs. Fitzlagen said with a wink. "Good luck to you finding that watch. And I hope you'll be feeling better soon. You must take care of yourself, you know. That's how wings break. They're not properly taken care of."

"Uh . . . sure," Molly said. "I will."

Mrs. Fitzlagen certainly said some odd things. Briefly, Molly pictured herself as having a broken wing and was shocked at how easily she could imagine it. She saw the picture vividly and held it in her mind's eye as she watched the tiny, red-haired woman make her way through the gravestones and into the woods.

Yes, Mrs. Fitzlagen was certainly strange. But Molly liked her.

Feeling a little better, Molly shook the image of her broken-winged self from her head and continued searching. After about a half hour, she gave up. The watch was simply gone. Perhaps some bird or other animal, a hedgehog or something, had gone off with it. She didn't know, but it wasn't there.

Her head ached again and she knew she'd better return to the castle. By the time she'd made it up the path, her hands trembled and her hair was damp with perspiration. No one seemed to be around, so she went into the castle and up to her room.

Getting out of her clothing, Molly put on her lacy white nightgown with the full, ruffled sleeves and climbed into bed. In an instant she was asleep. She awakened hours later as pink dusky light poured in through the narrow window. A tray lay on her bedside table with a steaming bowl of vegetable soup on it. Molly felt too groggy and tired to eat. She turned over and fell back asleep.

When she awakened again, it was night. Ashley lay asleep beside her and Katie was sleeping in her bed. The room was illuminated with the bright rays of a full moon. Sitting up, Molly looked at the moonlight and realized that its soft, wavery light might be caused by her slightly blurry vision. Her head felt a lot better, though. And, after her long sleep, she was no longer tired.

Tossing back her covers, she let her bare feet drop to the cold stone floor and walked over to the window. Looking out at the ocean, she watched the waves crest and break in silver lines of moonlight. Then something in the courtyard below caught her attention. Something dark and large moved.

With her forehead against the glass, Molly peered down into the yard. The shadowy thing stepped into a wide path of brilliant moonlight and Molly gasped.

Lucky Feather was loose. He must have somehow gotten out of the stable and come up to the courtyard. "Oh, no!" she gasped. She turned from the window, about to run out of the room to alert her father.

She stopped cold, though, as her mind raced.

Maybe she shouldn't run to tell him. This might not be a bad thing at all. Not for her. In fact, it might actually be lucky.

If she could be the one to keep Lucky Feather from wandering off, her father wouldn't be angry with her anymore.

How could he be?

She'd have saved his investment.

It occurred to Molly that this might even be the answer to her prayers. A chance for her to make everything right with her father. She imagined herself leading the horse back, her father at the stable, beside himself. He'd see how she'd saved the horse and wrap her in a hug. Molly would be a hero.

Looking back down at the courtyard, she watched as the horse pranced in the moonlight, tossing his black mane and tail as the wind tossed the bare trees. It looked cold. But she'd only be outside a few minutes. Lucky Feather and she understood one another. She'd be able to handle him. But she'd have to catch him quickly before he got out of the courtyard.

Sticking her bare feet into a pair of loafers, Molly pulled on her robe and ran out the bedroom door.

13

The wind tugged Molly's hair behind her as she stepped out into the moonlit courtyard. When Lucky Feather saw her, he stopped his moonstruck cavorting and nickered softly.

Slowly, carefully she approached him. "Nice boy, good boy," she crooned, urging him to stay where he was. He whinnied and shook his head at her, as if to say he couldn't be so easily tricked.

Lucky Feather wasn't saddled. Molly wondered how she would catch hold of him even if he did allow her to get close enough. If she could take hold of his mane, maybe she could lead him back to the stable. Or ride him bareback, steering him with her hands and legs.

The wind kicked up her nightclothes and she had to bat them back down. She glanced up at the startlingly white clouds rolling across the sky. The piercingly bright moon hung low in the sky as if it had decided to come down to earth for a visit.

This is crazy, she thought as Lucky Feather danced

before her, bathed in the shifting silver glow of moonlight. *I can't do this all alone. I have to get someone to help me.*

She looked back at the towering castle. The moon illuminated the stone facade, but the black windows were like closed eyes. Everyone was asleep inside. By the time she ran back for help, Lucky Feather might bolt and be gone forever.

She'd have made another bad decision, letting Lucky Feather go while she ran for help. That's how her father would see it. She could hear his incredulous, scornful, *angry* voice in her mind. "You just left him standing there, Molly? And you're always telling me how well you handle horses. It's your fault he's gone. You could have saved him but you didn't. You had to go running for help."

Molly couldn't stand to hear those words for real. No, and she wasn't going to hear them. She was going to bring Lucky Feather in. By herself.

"Lucky Feather, good boy," she crooned, continuing on. He dipped his head and looked up at her with fathomless black eyes. As their eyes met, again Molly felt that force, like a current of electricity jumping from Lucky Feather to herself. She moved closer. She wasn't really advancing on him, though. Rather, this mysterious horse was reeling her in, drawing her to him.

When she was just an arm's length away, Molly reached forward to touch him. Their eyes met and once again she felt that surge of deep communication.

Then, abruptly, unexpectedly, Lucky Feather took off at a gallop. Molly stared with wild, wide eyes as he careened down the length of the courtyard and bounded over the stone fence. For a moment, he seemed to hang in the air like some great, black Pegasus. Then he was gone.

Molly raced to the fence and leaned over it as far as she could. She was just in time to see Lucky Feather crashing down the narrow path that led to the graveyard.

A searing line of terrific pain flashed across Molly's forehead. She jammed the palm of her hand just above her nose to make it stop. In a moment, the pain subsided. Was she well enough to go after Lucky Feather? she wondered.

It didn't matter whether she was well enough or not. There was no one else to do it.

She had to go. It no longer seemed that important to corral her father's investment. It was Lucky Feather himself. She was genuinely worried Lucky Feather would hurt himself on that narrow path leading to the rocky shore. There was no time to call for help. In the time it would take her to go back and get help, Lucky Feather might disappear or . . . or hurt himself dreadfully. Molly had to save him.

Molly jumped over the fence and heard the sound of fabric tearing as her feet hit the dirt. The bottom ruffle of her lacy nightgown had snagged on a piece of jagged stone. A white flag of material whipped back and forth behind her. Molly didn't have time to care. She had to go after Lucky Feather.

The moonlight lit her path as she ran after the horse. She could hear the clatter of his hooves in the distance. Brambles caught at her robe, pricking it with their thorns. Freeing it took too much time. Finally, she slipped out of the robe, leaving it behind. A blast of cold air ran up her back, but she could stand it. Her movement and her eagerness to catch Lucky Feather would help keep her warm.

As Molly pushed on down the dirt path, the bare branches and thorns continued to snare her. Each time she impatiently yanked her nightgown free.

All the while, she kept listening for Lucky Feather's hoofbeats. It was the only way she'd be able to keep track of him. Did he have a destination? Or was he just running, enchanted with the moonlight and his own freedom?

Molly reached the graveyard just in time to see Lucky Feather soar over a gravestone on his way out the far end of the cemetery. Darting past the white stones and monuments, Molly hesitated for the slightest moment by her grandmother's kneeling angel. The moonlight illuminated the angel's gloriously radiant face, making it seem to glow from within. Her expression was so luminous she looked alive. For a moment, Molly hesitated, transfixed by the sight of her.

But she couldn't stop. She had to keep going. She pushed on, tearing her eyes from the angel and heading into the woods after Lucky Feather.

Soon the sound of crashing waves obscured Lucky Feather's hoofbeats. Molly followed the path to the cliff where, looking down, she saw the horse racing in circles on the beach. The sand shone as brightly as if a spotlight had been turned on it.

Molly put her hand to her head as a sudden spell of

dizziness rocked her. She staggered back a moment, bracing herself against a tree with one outstretched arm. After a moment, the dizziness passed. Relieved, she saw that Lucky Feather was still down on the beach.

Scrambling down the cliff, she came out onto the shore. Here, by the water, the cold was more intense as the wind blew a freezing ocean spray directly at her. Lucky Feather stopped his circular run and raced off along the shoreline.

Molly tried to follow him, but quickly lost sight of him again. As she looked at the shimmering wet sand in order to follow his hoofprints, she saw that the same, odd human footprints from the other day were *still* visible in the sand. At least they seemed to be the same prints.

The trail led along the cliff in the same direction they'd gone the day before. The tide washed in, lapping at her feet as she made her way along the base of the cliff. She worried, remembering how fast and high it had risen the other day. It would be dangerous to be caught out here if it rose that quickly again.

It would be dangerous for Lucky Feather, too. Would he be swept away and lost forever?

Looking over her shoulder, Molly briefly considered turning back. Then Lucky Feather neighed and she whirled around. His voice sounded close. But where was he? He wasn't on the beach ahead.

Another neigh enabled her to locate him. "Oh, my . . ." she murmured in amazement, her hand flying up to cover her gaping mouth.

Ahead of her, past the cave and around the bend in the cliff, was a stone jetty stretching out into the churning ocean. Lucky Feather stood at the very end of the jetty, silver waves spraying up on either side of him.

How had he gotten out there? How had he maneuvered on the slippery, uneven stones? One wrong move and he could have been plunged into the ocean.

Molly lifted her nightgown and knotted it at the side so it wouldn't be in her way. Then she headed toward the jetty. Waves sprayed her, plastering her hair to her head and soaking her gown as she stepped onto the first jetty rock. *This isn't too bad*, she thought, moving cautiously forward, arms outstretched for balance. *I can do this.*

A wave slapped her from the right and soaked her with icy water. She forced herself not to panic. If she lost her balance now, it would be a disaster.

But as she continued along the jetty, coming ever closer to the horse who seemed to be waiting for her at the end, a strange giddiness crept over her. What she was doing was completely crazy. Totally dangerous and insane. Yet, oddly enough, it made her want to laugh.

She did. She laughed out loud as another frigid wave hit her.

Stop it, Molly, she silently scolded. *This isn't funny!*

No. It wasn't funny. She wasn't laughing because she was amused. She was laughing because an odd happiness had taken hold of her. She didn't understand it, but it felt very real. Was this what people meant when they said someone was loony? She was freezing, trembling—and yet she felt at one with the entire world—with Lucky Feather, with the ocean, with the hovering moon. Completely at one.

At the end of the jetty, Lucky Feather waited. What

would he do when she reached him? she wondered. There was nowhere for him to run now. She'd simply have to lead him back. It wouldn't be easy, but he was an amazing horse and he'd made it out here. They'd make it back. Together.

Lucky Feather whinnied when she reached him and cast her a soulful glance. She smiled at him and, at that moment, something caught her eye.

Across the face of the full moon passed three black silhouettes, floating gracefully. She stared hard at them and it looked to her like they were winged creatures. *Angels*, she murmured. Angels passing across the moon.

It was so beautiful. What did it mean?

Molly turned back to Lucky Feather. They'd better go now, while they still had a chance.

But Molly needed one last look at the angels silhouetted by the moon. She looked back and was suddenly seized with a strong desire to join them, to be with them there, so close to the moon. She lifted up her right hand. She wanted to actually touch the moon. Shutting her eyes, she let the moonlight shine down on her. She felt as if she were soaking up its mysterious rays. She was somehow becoming energized by the light.

When Molly opened her eyes again, she blinked hard. Across the moon drifted three small silver clouds. They weren't angels at all. They never had been.

Or had they? They'd looked so real a moment ago.

Molly continued along the jetty, carefully planning each step from one dark, silver-rimmed rock to the next. For awhile she became absorbed in her own footfalls, concentrating on each carefully chosen step. Realizing she'd been looking at her feet for too long, she raised her head to check on Lucky Feather.

As she did, a wall of icy water rose up and smashed into her.

With a blast of numbing cold, it tossed her high in the air, only to drop her again into the ocean's frigid, churning blackness.

14

The shock of the water sent Molly reeling. Down she plunged, down below the surface of the water, helpless to halt her downward tumble, her arms and legs spread wide, her nightgown ballooning around her.

Engulfed in the jet black water, she continued to sink until her momentum finally slowed and she drifted.

Drifted . . . drifted . . .

Then, slowly, Molly began to rise.

The sharp, deep breath she'd taken just before going under now ached to be released and replaced with another. She couldn't let it out, though. There *was* no other breath waiting to take its place. Numb with shock and cold, she could hardly think at all, but she couldn't exhale, that much she knew.

Lungs bursting, Molly began swimming with all her strength. But the water was so black. Was she even swimming up?

Her sense of direction was gone. Maybe she was swimming down.

In another minute it wouldn't matter. Her last breath would escape. Water would rush in to take its place in her starved lungs.

Molly felt something brush against her leg. A fish? Hands? Could it be?

Yes. Impossibly soft, strong hands grasped Molly above her knees and sped her up, up. She twisted, writhing to see who was lifting her. It was too dark, though. She couldn't see anything. But whoever—whatever—it was moving with incredible speed.

In seconds she broke the water's surface. Drinking in great gulps of air, Molly flailed desperately.

A wave washed over her, pushing her under, but this time she was able to fight her way back to the surface. Another wave smacked her in the face, filling up her nose and her mouth.

Why had her mysterious helper deserted her now? Why had she been saved only to drown here in the pounding waves?

"Molly! Molly!" A wind-whipped voice fought its way to her. "Molly!"

A small boat, sails flapping madly, was approaching. "Molly!"

It was her father.

Struggling with the swinging sails, he managed to bring the boat alongside her. He reached over the side and grabbed her arms. With surprising strength he pulled her aboard.

Molly wanted to speak, but she was too overcome with cold and terror. Her father scooped her up in his arms and cradled her, rocking back and forth. "Oh,

Molly! Molly!" he sobbed. "My own dear child!"

In that moment, a giant wave washed over the boat. Molly felt her father's arms slip from her shoulders as she slid forward. The heavy metal boom to the mainsail swung wildly around. "Look out!" Molly yelled.

Her father turned.

Too late. With a sickening crack, the boom hit his head and sent him flying out of the boat.

"Dad!" Molly screamed. She reached out for him. His hand was still visible above the surface of the choppy water.

Molly grabbed a rope from the bottom of the boat and hurled it into the water. It fell close to his hand. "Grab the rope!" she yelled as the boat pitched back and forth dangerously. "The rope, Dad! I'll save you!"

Could he hear her? Why wasn't he struggling, trying to swim?

"Nooo!" she screamed in anguish as his hand slipped beneath the surface. The boom must have knocked him out. He couldn't swim back. He was unconscious.

Molly leaned out of the boat as wave after wave washed over her. "Dad!" she called. Maybe he was under there and coming awake. He'd need to follow the sound of her voice to find the surface. Maybe her voice would even reach him, awaken him.

"Dad! Wake up! Wake up! Dad! Swim up! Swim up to me! Swim to . . ."

Molly hung her head in defeat and slumped back in the boat as it rocked violently back and forth.

Was her father gone? Had he died trying to save her?

No. No, he couldn't be. He couldn't be dead. She

pulled herself back up and looked over the side of the boat. She scanned the churning ocean but saw nothing.

The boat pitched violently, nearly dumping her back into the water. Molly gripped the side of the boat as another wave washed over, then shifted quickly to the other side to counterweight the boat. She had no idea how to sail. Even if she did, the water was too rough. She'd never make it.

Suddenly, Molly noticed something had changed. The boat wasn't rocking anymore. There was singing. And music.

A flute.

Molly looked up and her eyes went wide despite the almost blinding white light.

The boat's sails had dropped. Taking their place were three tall angels.

Their silver-white gowns billowed like sails. Their gleaming, feathery wings vibrated at an incredible speed so that they didn't appear to be moving at all—like a hummingbird's wings—yet Molly could feel the warm, powerful breeze they created.

The first angel faced front and looped her flowing white sleeve around the center pole, acting like a jib sail, her gown full of wind, her long, black hair swept back.

Behind her, a second angel spread his gown wide to catch more wind.

Hovering above them, a blonde angel played a flute in mid-air.

The flute. Molly remembered Edwina playing the flute in the stream. Could it really be true? It was! It was Ned, Norma, and Edwina. They looked very different, but it *was* them. It had to be.

Ned and Norma were singing. Molly couldn't make out the words. They seemed to be in another language, one she'd never heard. Could it be Gaelic? The song was haunting, yet lovely. Something about the song sounded old, ancient.

The music had a quality that gave Molly courage. With its sound a resolve crept into her, seeping into her very bone.

They glided on the water for a short while before a final wave carried the boat in to settle gently on the rocky shore. The angels floated away from the boat. They hovered nearby, shimmering softly.

Using all her strength, Molly pulled herself out of the boat. "Please," she pleaded in a croaking, exhausted voice. "Please. My father. Please help him!"

The angels smiled gently at her. Their faces were warm and comforting, but they didn't seem to understand.

"Please," Molly sobbed, staggering forward, her body wracked with emotion. "Please. My father."

Was it her imagination, or were the angels rising? Slowly, they lifted into the air and drifted ever higher.

"No!" Molly shouted, reaching out to them. "Don't go. My father!"

The angels continued to float up.

"Wait! My father . . . my . . ." Molly's knees gave way. Her arms flailed helplessly as the earth whirled beneath her feet. Soon everything went black.

15

Molly's eyes opened to blinding sunlight and the sound of steady pounding. She blinked hard. As she did, she realized something ice-cold was tickling her toes.

Propping herself on her elbows, she looked down. Of course! The pounding and the cold came from the foaming white surf as it crashed to shore and washed over her bare feet. She rubbed her eyes and realized her hands were covered with gritty brown sand.

Stiff and achy, Molly leaned forward. She saw her blonde hair was encrusted in sand and ribbons of dried seaweed.

Slowly, the events of the night before came back to her and she let out an anguished sob when she remembered how her father had been lost, trying to save her. Burying her face in her sandy hands, she cried deep wracking sobs.

Despite his coldness and his criticism, she loved him. He was her father.

She'd always loved him, that's why it hurt so much

that he thought so little of her. But he didn't think so little of her. He didn't! He wasn't cold! He loved her, too. She knew that now. He'd risked his life to save her.

And it was all her fault. Her fault! Why had she thought she could ever catch Lucky Feather? She knew why. Because she was desperate to make things right between her father and herself.

She wondered what had happened to Lucky Feather. Had he, too, been swept out to sea?

She sat and looked out at the deep green of the now calm ocean. Slowly, it occurred to her that maybe her father wasn't dead. He might have survived, just as she, too, had survived.

Standing, she shielded her eyes with one hand and scanned the ocean and the beach. "Dad," she whispered. "Dad, please hold on. Someone's coming to help you. I'm coming. Don't give up, Dad. I love you, Dad. Hang on. Please. Please."

Keeping her eyes on the water for any sign of him, she bit her lip. Hard. She felt so helpless, so useless. He was knocked unconscious. He had fallen into frigid water. He must be . . . he must be . . . dead.

Tears rolled down Molly's cheeks, each tear a pain-filled capsule escaping from deep inside her. So much pain! Endless, ever-flowing. That's how it felt. So much sadness that if she didn't get it out, it might shatter her frail body and scatter it to the winds.

Finally, though, the tears stopped. She felt hollow inside. Empty. With vacant eyes, she stared out at the ocean for a long time. The tide washed in, covering her legs, but she didn't notice or care. What did it matter now?

After a long while, a green bottle washed up at her feet. She glanced at it and then looked away, disinterested. But it bobbed persistently in front of her, as if demanding her attention.

Looking at it dully, she watched it bob. It seemed like a bottle specially delivered by the ocean. The glass shimmered in the morning light and Molly slowly realized it was familiar to her.

Picking it up, she remembered. This was the same kind of bottle she'd seen lined up in the cave the other day. Each with its message inside.

This one had a message, too. A small yellowed paper lay in a scroll at the bottom. Molly uncorked the bottle and shook out the paper. It came out easily this time. Unrolling it, she read the message scrawled in a childish script.

> Help me, someone. I'm about to be imprisoned at The Edgarton Boarding School in London. It's like a horrible nightmare. Father says I must go. I fear he doesn't want me around anymore. If you get this note, please come and help me escape. I won't cause you any trouble. My mom is dead. She was my best friend. I need help desperately. Thank you in advance. Ian Morgan. 1959.

Ian Morgan! Molly stared at the name. What was this? How could this be? Had her father really written this? In

1959? Had this bottle floated in the ocean all these years just to be delivered to his very own daughter on this very morning? What could it mean?

Had an invisible hand swept it to her?

Molly remembered the angels.

Why had they saved her and not her father? It made no sense.

Maybe they *had* saved him. If he were alive, it would be a miracle. But wasn't it a miracle that she, herself, was alive? Perhaps he'd washed ashore and was lying there not far from her.

Still holding the green bottle, Molly stood and began walking down the beach. The sun was blinding and she walked with her head down. Surprisingly, she actually felt better than she had the day before. Her muscles were no longer stiff. Her head didn't ache.

"Come on, Dad. Hang on now. I'm going to find you and you're going to be okay. I will find you, Dad. Don't worry," she said quietly as she walked. Somehow she felt it was important to talk. She wasn't sure why. Maybe her voice, her energy, would be a lifeline for him. It didn't make sense, but she felt it. And, besides, what else could she do?

The sharp *caw* of a bird caught her attention and she looked up sharply. Three large white gulls swooped in a circle overhead. They were looking down at something. She looked to see what—and gasped.

A flat skiff motored toward her, lightly skipping over the waves.

In it, running the small outboard motor, stood a glorious figure in a billowing gown of light green. Her wild red hair blew behind her on the ocean breeze. Her white feathered wings fluttered in the wind.

As the boat came nearer, Molly could see a hand hanging limply over the side. A man's large hand.

Her father!

The angel was bringing her father home!

Molly dropped the bottle in the sand and ran out through the breaking surf to meet the boat. Now she could hear the drone of its motor. Her awe of the angel was overcome by the stronger desire to see her father. She looked out and the sunlight hit her full in the face. Turning away, she shielded her eyes.

"Help me with this boat, Molly," called a familiar voice. "Please."

Looking back, she saw tiny Mrs. Fitzlagen standing in the boat.

She gaped in surprise. Mrs. Fitzlagen? Had she been seeing things before? Or was Mrs. Fitzlagen really an angel?

"Hurry, girl. I need your help here," Mrs. Fitzlagen said, her sharp tone snapping Molly from her stunned daze.

Molly waded out until she was up to her waist in the breaking surf. Mrs. Fitzlagen had turned off the motor. "Steady the boat," she instructed. "Hold onto it."

Grasping hold of the side, Molly helped keep the boat steady as the waves pushed it in to shore. Funny, she thought, how she would know her father's hand so well.

When the boat was securely on shore, Molly stared at her father's limp form slumped in the boat. How pale he looked, his dark disheveled hair framing his face. His expression was slack and peaceful. For the first time ever she saw in him the trusting, scared, innocent boy who had written the note in the bottle. It seemed to her now that the person she knew—the person she thought he was—had simply been a mask, a fake.

Molly jumped into the boat and put her ear to his chest. Nothing. "I don't hear a heartbeat," she said. "We have to do something."

Mrs. Fitzlagen gently pulled her away from her father. Then she sat on Mr. Morgan's broad chest and pushed down with her arms several times. She didn't seem to exert much effort. Molly was frightened that she wasn't strong enough.

Mrs. Fitzlagen knew what Molly was feeling. "Don't worry, child," she said as she pushed. "I'm a fixer of broken hearts. Remember?" She leaned down and listened, then moved to his side and opened wide his slack jaw.

"Aren't you supposed to tilt his head back," Molly offered anxiously.

"I have my own ways," Mrs. Fitzlagen replied. "He won't be the first I've saved." She knelt and blew into his mouth like a child blowing the round, white puff of an autumn dandelion.

Mr. Morgan's eyes slowly fluttered open.

"Dad!" Molly sobbed.

"Molly," he replied, his voice hoarse and raspy. He reached up for her. "My Molly."

She knelt and took his hand, gripping it tightly. Mr. Morgan squeezed back and then his head slumped forward and his eyes shut.

Molly's eyes darted to Mrs. Fitzlagen in alarm.

"He's fine now," Mrs. Fitzlagen assured her. "The danger is over. He's breathing again. Poor fellow. He hung there in between the two worlds a long time. It's hard on the body, that hanging in between is. It's exhausted him."

Mrs. Fitzlagen gazed down at Molly's father and shook her head sadly. "He looks like he did as a boy. Such a shame that he grew up to be the man his father wanted him to be," she said. "Things would have been different if his mother had lived. She shielded him from his father's sternness. She saw how sensitive he was and how much the art was in him."

"The art?" Molly asked.

"Ah, yes. Your father was always painting and sketching. It was his dream to be an artist. But his father would have nothing of it. He pressured the boy into studying economics. He was smart and mastered it, but it killed him inside. All these years he's been walking around nearly dead inside because he didn't follow his heart."

"Nearly dead inside," Molly repeated. Molly's mind raced as she remembered the sketches she'd found in his desk drawer. He'd done them! Of course. It was clear now, but she'd never have suspected her father had artistic ability like that. And the sketchbook—the one she'd found in the cave.

"Yes," Mrs. Fitzlagen said, reading her thoughts. "He did those sketches when he was just a boy. That was his place. His secret place."

Molly looked hard at Mrs. Fitzlagen. "Were you his . . . his . . . angel?"

"The Beirne family has always been dear to me, yes," she replied. "But they've forgotten."

"Forgotten you?"

"Forgotten what's in their hearts. When you lose track of your heart, you lose track of your angel."

Molly studied her father's pale face. He'd forgotten his angel. How sad. But maybe she was the same. He'd given up on his art, and she was about to give up on being an astronaut because her parents didn't want her to do it—just as his father hadn't wanted him to be an artist. Would she, too, wind up cold and distant, wearing a mask to cover her real self?

"There she is!" The urgent voice made Molly look up. Mr. and Mrs. Kingsley were coming down the cliff. Christina, Ashley, and Katie were just ahead of them, hurrying down as fast as the difficult climb would allow.

She turned to Mrs. Fitzlagen. Where was she? Looking in every direction, Molly realized she'd disappeared. All that remained was a trail of bare footprints running along the shoreline, prints that the surf didn't erase.

"Molly, are you okay?" Katie shouted. The first to reach the beach, she ran across the sand toward Molly, Christina and Ashley close behind.

What good friends they were. Molly was so glad to see them. She stood, wanting to assure them she was unhurt, everything was okay. As she climbed out of the boat, she began to tremble uncontrollably. Suddenly everything that had happened—the fall, Lucky Feather, the physical strain of her near drowning, her amazing encounter with angels, the awful, sudden loss of her father and his miraculous return—it all overwhelmed her.

And the sun. The sun was so blinding!

The surf rang loudly in Molly's ears as she fell to the ground in a faint.

When Molly opened her eyes again, Christina, Ashley, and Katie were staring down at her with alarmed expressions. Mrs. Kingsley knelt at her side, tapping her cheeks. "Wake up, honey," she was saying softly but insistently. "Wake up."

16

The next thing Molly saw was her father.

Mr. Morgan sat up in the boat. Molly rushed to him, throwing her arms around him. "Dad! Dad!" she cried, burying her face in his shoulder and inhaling the redolent smell of deep ocean water. "Dad!"

He put his arm around her and rested his head on hers. He seemed weak, worn out. "It's all right, baby. It's all right," he said in a gravelly voice she barely recognized. His voice was raw, as if he'd swallowed buckets of sea water.

Molly looked up into his face. His eyes were red-rimmed and his face was scratched. Mrs. Fitzlagen said he'd hung in between worlds a long time. Had he drowned and been brought back? Molly would never know.

But he *was* back and that was what mattered. Molly hugged her father as tightly as she could.

He laughed self-consciously, but then he hugged her back, gripping her tightly.

They clung together that way for several minutes. "I heard your voice, Molly," he murmured.

She pulled away and looked at him hard. "You did?"

He nodded, his eyes taking on a faraway expression. "I awoke in a strange place—or maybe I dreamed it, I don't know which. It was bluish gray. There was nothing there but a light, a white light blinking on and off way in the distance. I got up to go toward it, but I heard your voice. You were calling me and I had to get back to you, so I turned away from the light. The next thing I knew, I felt a strong wind and then I was staring up at your wonderful face."

"I *was* calling you," Molly said quietly. "I was calling you forever."

Again, her father nodded, as if this made sense to him. "I'm glad you did."

"We'd better get the two of you out of here," Mr. Kingsley said. "You both need to see a doctor."

"I'm fine," Mr. Morgan said as he attempted to pull himself up. He got halfway and then faltered. Mrs. Kingsley caught him, gripping his arm.

"Ian, don't push yourself. You were unconscious for a while," Mrs. Kingsley reminded him. "That's never a good thing. And Molly was out here all night. Just look at her."

All eyes turned to Molly as she sat next to her father in her torn white nightgown, her hopelessly tangled hair filled with sand and seaweed.

"What happened?" Christina asked.

"Lucky Feather got loose and—" Molly began.

"Not now," Mrs. Kingsley interrupted. "Tell us later, after you've both rested. It's easy to see you've both been through an ordeal. Let's get you back to the castle, first."

Mr. Kingsley helped Mr. Morgan to his feet. Christina put her arm around Molly and Molly leaned on her as they began to walk down the shore. Molly was amazed at how totally exhausted she suddenly felt.

Ashley picked up the green bottle stuck in the sand. "Hey, here's one of those bottles we saw the other day. And there's a note in this one, too. We left this back in the cave. How did it get here?"

Molly glanced at her father, wondering if he'd recognize the bottle. He stared at it, frowning thoughtfully, but didn't say anything.

"Do you want me to bring it?" Ashley asked, holding up the bottle.

"Yes, please," Molly said as Mrs. Kingsley helped her out of the boat. "I'd like to keep it."

*   *   *

At the castle, Katie, Christina, and Ashley helped Molly get cleaned up. Mrs. Loughlin made trip after trip bringing warm water in a kettle to fill the bath. "Bah! Those old pipes," she'd said scornfully. Nothing would do but for her to haul the water herself.

While Molly soaked in lavender-scented bubbles, she heard sounds outside in the hallway. Ashley poked her head in. "We're helping Mrs. Loughlin build a fire so the room will be cozy when you get out."

Molly smiled at her. "Thanks." Washing the sand, bits of shell, and seaweed out of her hair was such an effort that she felt weak afterward. She climbed out of the tub and dried herself on the fluffy cream-colored towels

Mrs. Loughlin had laid out just for her. She slipped into a thick terrycloth robe produced by the redoubtable Mrs. Loughlin and toddled back to her room.

The room was bright and warm with the roaring fire Mrs. Loughlin and the girls had set. "Come on, get right into bed," Christina said as soon as Molly entered.

Molly settled into a bed of crisp, warm, fresh sheets. Mrs. Loughlin came in and tucked a hot water bottle wrapped in green flannel into the bed with her. It was surprisingly comforting.

"I'll get you some hot tea and biscuits," Mrs. Loughlin said kindly. "I'll just be a moment. You'll be wanting some soup, too, I imagine. I'll bring it."

"Thank you," Molly said, falling back into the plump pillows.

Sitting beside her on the bed, Katie, Ashley, and Christina set to work combing out Molly's tangled hair. "What was in the bottle? What happened?" Katie asked as she combed Molly's hair.

"I have the bottle. I'll be right back," Ashley said, leaving the bed. She returned holding the green bottle with the rolled-up paper inside. "I read the message," she said. "I just had to. I can't believe it was from your father. That's just too strange. Where did this bottle come from? Did you go back to the cave for it?"

"No, it washed up right at my feet," Molly said, taking the bottle from her. "I swear. That's exactly what happened."

Christina's eyes widened. "That is more than a coincidence," she said confidently. "You know what? I've been thinking about the stone angel and the footprints.

Do you think that somehow angels were involved in getting this bottle to you?"

"I think so," Molly said as she leaned forward. "I know so, really. Last night I saw angels."

"You did?" Ashley gasped.

Molly nodded. "You know Mrs. Fitzlagen?"

"Scoot now," Mrs. Loughlin said, coming into the room with a cup of tea and a bowl of something steaming. "This girl needs to rest."

"She's an angel," Ashley finished in an awed, breathless voice.

"What did you say?" Mrs. Loughlin asked, glaring suspiciously.

Ashley smiled and patted her arm. "I said you're an angel, Mrs. Loughlin."

The elderly woman smiled radiantly. "Why, thank you," she said, handing Molly a bowl of delicious-smelling broth. "Oxtail soup," she told Molly. "Eat it. It will do you good, it will." She left, shooing Ashley, Katie, and Christina out of the room with her.

As Molly was finishing her soup, a short, stocky man with thick white hair knocked on the door and entered.

"I'm Doctor Maloney," he said with a heavy brogue. "I hear you took a tumble in the Atlantic. Let's have a look at you." He examined Molly, grunting to himself and nodding. Then he stood back and studied her with a serious expression, absently patting the pockets of his worn tweed suit. "You're too thin," he told her bluntly. "Don't you like to eat?"

Molly shrugged. "Yeah. Sure. I'm just not always hungry."

"Well, eat. You're a pretty young girl, not a skeleton. Now then, suppose you tell me what happened last night."

Molly didn't know where to begin. She couldn't tell a complete stranger about the angels. "I was chasing a horse and I fell in the water. My father tried to save me but then he fell in, too. I guess we both washed ashore."

"Chasing a horse, eh?" the doctor asked. "In the middle of the night?"

Molly nodded.

"And did you catch the horse, then?"

"No. No," Molly said, sadly thinking of poor Lucky Feather buffeted by waves there in the dark. "But maybe he washed ashore, too. I hope so but I don't know."

The doctor scrutinized her. "That's a pretty wild story, though you don't seem to be in shock, which was what I wanted to find out."

Molly was glad she hadn't told him about the angels. He'd probably have rushed her to the hospital.

"I'd say you've survived your near drowning with almost unbelievable good luck," he said. "You're fine. But I want you to rest for the next two days. And don't go chasing any more horses in the middle of the night." The doctor winked at her jauntily. "Promise?"

Molly smiled. "Promise."

He put his hand on the doorknob to leave but lingered a moment, looking at her. "The angels must be on your side, my girl. Your father's, too. I don't know how the two of you survived the night, what with the cold and all."

"I think they are," Molly said with a small smile. If he only knew how right he was.

The doctor left and Molly fell back onto her pillows, quickly falling into a deep, dreamless sleep.

She awoke again to the sound of her door opening. It was night now, and the fire in the hearth had settled down to a low, crackling glow. Her father slowly entered her room, throwing a wavering shadow across the floor.

"Oh, you're awake," he said, coming to her bedside. Once again, his voice was deep and resonant, yet it retained a slightly raspy sound, as if he hadn't quite washed all the salt and grit of the ocean from his throat.

"Yes, I just woke up," Molly replied, turning toward him groggily. "How are *you* feeling?"

"A little shaky still, but fine," he said as he sat on the edge of her bed. He took her hand in his. He'd never before made this sort of affectionate gesture. Small as it was, it filled Molly's heart with warmth.

"Molly, are you well enough to tell me what happened?" he asked calmly.

With a rush of anxiety, Molly thought about Lucky Feather. She'd lost the investment. Maybe if she hadn't gone after him, Lucky Feather would have simply wandered back to the stable. Maybe none of this would have happened. Would her father be angry at her when he heard the truth, as angry as he'd been when she'd tried to ride Lucky Feather? Yet he kept hold of her hand and there was a new softness in his voice. Something in it told her she could talk to him honestly.

"Lucky Feather got loose," she began, then continued on to tell how she'd followed him out onto the jetty and fallen in. "How did you find me?" she asked.

"I woke up because the shutter outside my window

was loose and banging," he said. "I went to the window and saw you running across the courtyard in the moonlight."

A picture leaped into Molly's head. She imagined an angel outside her father's window, a beautiful winged angel banging a shutter to wake him up.

"You saw Lucky Feather, too?" she asked.

"No. I only saw you."

"That must have been after he leaped over the fence," Molly mused aloud.

"Lucky Feather was there?" Mr. Morgan said. "You're sure?"

"Of course. That's why I was out of my room. Lucky Feather got loose and I wanted to bring him back. You must have seen him at some time last night."

Mr. Morgan shook his head. "I didn't know what you were doing down there. I went down to tell you to come inside—it was too cold to be running about in your night clothes—but you were gone. I followed the path and found your robe caught in the bushes. Then I found scraps of your nightgown. Once I reached the graveyard, I guessed you'd gone down to the ocean."

"Didn't you see Lucky Feather out on the jetty then? You must have." Molly insisted. How could he have not seen him?

"No, only you. You were the only one I saw."

How odd. Why hadn't he seen Lucky Feather? "Where did you get the sailboat?" she asked.

A quizzical, faraway look came into his eyes. "It was the strangest thing. I saw you slip and was desperate to reach you, but had no idea how to do it. Then I came upon this strange small woman on the shore. By the light of the moon, she was mending the torn sail of a boat, sewing it. I ran to her, but before I could say anything, she hoisted the sails and said, 'Hurry.'"

"Did you know the woman?" Molly asked, sure it had been Mrs. Fitzlagen.

"She was so familiar. I know I've seen her before. But where could I possibly know her from? Perhaps it was from my boyhood, long ago, when we lived here."

"Maybe," Molly agreed. She reached over and pulled open the drawer in her bedside table. She took out the sketchbook she'd found. "Is this from your boyhood, too?" she asked, handing it to him.

He opened the book and stared at it in amazement. "This is mine, yes. Where did you ever find this?"

Molly told him about the cave, how she'd spotted the light burning inside.

"That lantern can't still be burning after all these years!" he exclaimed, astonished.

"It must be," Molly replied. "That woman, the one who gave you that boat. She's Mrs. Fitzlagen. She helped us get out of the cave before the tide came in."

"Oh, my heavens," he gasped. "That's right. The tide. You could have drowned. Thank God for Mrs. Fitzlagen. You've spoken to her, then."

"She was mending the wing on grandmother's angel the other day. That's when I met her."

Mr. Morgan suddenly went pale. "Mrs. Fitzlagen," he murmured. "I remember now. She was my mother's friend. I would sometimes see my mother and Mrs. Fitzlagen talking down on the beach." An anguished, far-off look came into his eyes. "When my mother was very sick, dying really, she told me that if I ever needed anything, I could count on Mrs. Fitzlagen. I'd forgotten all about her. But wait! How could that be? The woman looks exactly the same now as I remember her looking then. It's impossible. Could it be her daughter?"

"No. That's her," Molly assured him. "That's *the* Mrs. Fitzlagen."

"Why do you say that? How can you be sure?"

Molly sat up and put her free hand on his arm. She felt she could confide in him now as never before. "Dad, Mrs. Fitzlagen is an angel. She saved your life. She brought you in to shore on that boat. She breathed life into you."

"Yes, of course, she is a dear. An angel, as you say. Thank goodness she was there. I must find her and thank her for saving my life. But it doesn't explain why she looks the same now as she did so many years ago. That must be her daughter. It must be."

"No, Dad," Molly said. "I don't mean she's an angel, like a sweet person. I mean she's an angel."

"What?"

"The kind with wings."

Mr. Morgan stared at her, stunned. Then he scowled. "No. It couldn't be. Why that's just . . ." His voice trailed off and he frowned as if he were remembering something.

"What is it?" Molly asked.

"When I was in the . . . place . . . the in-between place, I just remembered that someone was with me. It was . . . it was an . . ."

"Angel?" Molly finished inquiringly.

"Yes," he said, his voice almost a whisper, "a gorgeous, red-haired angel. And I'd seen her before, when I was a boy."

"Mrs. Fitzlagen," Molly said. "They saved me, too. Not Mrs. Fitzlagen, but other angels," Molly told him.

"Angels," he said as if he were still absorbing the idea. Abruptly, he opened the sketchpad. His eyes lingered a moment on the sketch of his mother, then he flipped to a page at the back of the book, one Molly hadn't noticed before.

"Mrs. Fitzlagen!" she cried, looking at it. "Then you did know her. This proves it. It's the same woman. The exact same woman."

"She posed for this the day after my mother died. I was so lonely, but I could always find Mrs. Fitzlagen on the beach. She was someone kind to talk to. An angel, though? It's simply too much to believe."

"She was there when you needed her, like your mother said."

"True," he conceded. "But then my father sent me to boarding school in England and . . . well . . ."

"You didn't want to go," Molly said, handing him the green bottle.

He took the bottle and shook out the note.

"I found it on the beach," she explained.

Mr. Morgan stared at the note, deep in thought. "This is truly amazing. You know, I sent this bottle out because I felt all alone. I was scared and desperate for someone to be close to."

"I know how that feels," Molly said quietly.

He stared at her. "I suppose you do," he said after a moment. "I see something now as I never saw it before. I treat you the way my father treated me. Almost exactly the same."

"Why?" Molly dared to ask.

"I don't know," he admitted. "I suppose I thought it was the way a father should be. But, you know, the moment I saw you slip from that jetty, everything changed. I thought, 'I'm going to lose this child who is so precious to me.' And suddenly it all became so clear. I distance myself from people. It's how I survived boarding school. It's a reflex. But to put distance between myself and my child—that's insane. To have lost you would have been . . . unthinkable."

"I love you, Dad," Molly said, tears of gladness in her eyes. She'd waited her whole life for this moment, to hear him say he cared, for him to explain why he acted the way he did.

"I love you, too, Molly."

Molly had never heard these words from him before, not spoken straight out like this. It made her heart soar with joy. Commander Demander had died at sea, and an angel had given her a father to love.

He put his arm around Molly, hugging her tightly to him. "It was such a crazy idea, looking for love by putting a note in a bottle. But—who would have guessed—it worked." He squeezed her emotionally. "It worked."

17

"So that's it," Molly said, sitting up in bed. She'd just finished telling her friends the complete story of what had happened to her.

"Wow! Mrs. Fitzlagen is an angel. Awesome," Christina said from her spot sitting cross-legged at the end of one bed. She looked around the room. "Guess what Mrs. Loughlin told me," she said. "Your dad told her to set this room up special for us. The fires, the canopied beds, even the desk. Wasn't that nice?"

"He did?" said Molly. "I didn't know that. That *was* pretty nice of him." Molly was still getting used to the idea of a father who'd cared all along. "Everything's turned out pretty great. The only sad part is Lucky Feather."

"What do you mean?" Ashley said. "Lucky Feather is fine. He's in the stable right this very minute."

"What? That's impossible," Molly cried. "Are you kidding?"

"No," Ashley said with a smile as she pulled a heavy

knit sweater over her head. "He's down in the stable. It was like he was never gone, except that the door to his stall and the front door of the stable were wide open."

Molly leaped out of bed. "Why didn't anyone tell me? I thought he was dead!"

"It wasn't that easy to talk to you yesterday," Katie said, bending to tie the laces of her tan workboots. "Everyone kept shooing us away and then you slept so much."

"Besides," Ashley added, "we didn't realize you thought he might be dead. We didn't exactly have the whole story until you told us just now."

Molly opened her suitcase and grabbed a haphazard pile of clothing. "I have to go see him. Now," she said as she pulled her jeans on under her nightgown. In an instant she was dressed and running out the door with Christina, Ashley, and Katie trailing behind her.

The adults were already having breakfast in the dining hall when she ran through. "Where are you going?" asked Mr. Morgan. "You're supposed to be resting."

"I feel fine," Molly said honestly, not stopping. "Lucky Feather is alive."

"Well, of course he's alive," Mr. Morgan murmured, bewildered. "Who said he wasn't?"

Molly ran down the stairs, through the back room, and out to the courtyard. It was a brilliant, sunny day with rolling white clouds against a vivid blue sky. She ran to the corner of the courtyard and found the path that led to the stable.

Molly hurried down the path until she came to a

lovely, low stone building with a red shingled roof and wide green wooden doors. Molly leaned her weight into one door and pushed it open.

There stood Lucky Feather. His gleaming, black grandeur dimmed not at all by his wild moonlight frolic. He looked at her, then nodded his head and whinnied a greeting.

Molly rushed to his stall and laid her hands on his warm, glossy neck. Somehow she needed to feel him to be sure he was real. He was.

She stared into his mysterious black eyes. "What are you?" she whispered. There seemed to be an answer in his eyes, but she couldn't read it.

"See, I told you," Ashley said, bursting through the doors. "He's as good as ever."

Katie and Christina came in behind her. They all joined Molly in Lucky Feather's stall. "Could a horse be an angel?" Molly asked, not caring that the question sounded ridiculous.

"I don't know," Katie said, frowning.

"Why not," Christina said, her voice overlapping Katie's. The two girls looked at one another and laughed.

"Who knows," Ashley said philosophically. "Angels can probably do about anything, change into anything, *be* anything." She patted Lucky Feather's flank. "Even if they can't be angels, I've always thought there was something mysterious about horses."

Molly stared at Lucky Feather. How had he made it on and off that jetty so quickly and safely? Had he deliberately led her on that crazy chase? And why? Why?

"An angel might have been riding him," Christina

suggested, as if reading Molly's thoughts. "Someone had to have let him out."

This idea captured Molly's imagination. It felt right to her somehow. She could tell her friends agreed. They looked at one another and nodded, awed by all the amazing possibilities they were considering.

Later that afternoon, Molly ventured into the woods by herself. She wanted to find Mrs. Fitzlagen's cottage again. She needed to thank her for all she'd done. But, although she was sure she remembered the exact location, she couldn't find the cottage. It seemed to have disappeared.

Hoping to find her in the graveyard, Molly went there. It was empty. She crossed to her grandmother's grave. "Thank you, Mrs. Fitzlagen. Wherever you are," she spoke to the air, firmly convinced Mrs. Fitzlagen would hear her. "I'll never forget you."

As she was about to turn back, something glinting in the sunlight caught her eye. The light came from the bowl the stone angel held. "My watch!" Molly gasped, seizing it with delight. "My watch."

A wind rustled the high grass around the gravestones and monuments, sending a ripple across it. Molly smiled as she clasped the watch to her wrist. She stopped and listened to the wind. That was when she noticed something. There was something missing, a background sound—like traffic on a distant highway—that had stopped.

It was loneliness. The loneliness she carried with her all the time. The loneliness she'd gotten used to. It was gone.

* * *

Molly ripped open the silver bag of chips Christina handed her and gazed out at the towering clouds. That morning they'd loaded Lucky Feather into a narrow horse trailer and brought him to Shannon International Airport in Limerick. From there they'd walked him up a ramp into the private plane Mr. Morgan had chartered. Lucky Feather had been somewhat skittish, especially when it came time to enter the special stall that had been fitted into the plane, but he hadn't been a lot of trouble to move.

"My ears are popping," Christina complained from the seat beside Molly. "Do you have any gum?"

"No, I'll ask my father. I saw him buy some in the airport." She got up and walked up the aisle to where her father sat, sketching on a pad propped against his knee. It was a sketch of the castle. "Nice," Molly commented.

"Thanks." He handed her some gum when she asked. "Mr. Kingsley and I talked earlier," he said. "I thought you might like to know that we'll be boarding Lucky Feather at the Pine Manor Ranch. So you'll be able to visit him— and maybe take a few cautious rides, too, eh?"

"Cool! Excellent!" Molly cried happily.

She looked at her friends. Katie was immersed in whatever music was coming over her headphones, writing diligently all the while in her black-and-white notebook. Ashley's eyes were squeezed shut in a desperate effort to sleep and block out the flying experience.

Molly went back to her seat and told Christina about Lucky Feather.

"Now that's destiny," she said.

"You think so?" Molly asked.

"Sure. Lucky Feather was meant to come into your life. And he's not leaving. Something tells me you and he are going to be extremely close."

Molly nodded, pleased to hear this. Christina and her hunches were seldom wrong.

Katie joined them and held out a page in her notebook. "Look what I just figured out," she said. Molly looked at the page. On it was written *Mrs. Fitzlagen*, below that, *Mrs. Fitzangel*. "It's like Nagle, my cat," Katie said.

"What?" Molly questioned.

"It's an anagram. *Lagen* is an anagram for *angel*."

"Wow, you're right," Molly agreed. It seemed so obvious now. "We should have realized it right away."

"Sometimes you don't see stuff that's right in front of you," Katie said, taking back her book. "It happens a lot."

" 'Though seeing, they do not see,' " Christina quoted.

Katie rolled her eyes. "What's that from? The *I Ching? The Tibetan Book of the Dead?* Today's horoscope?"

Christina smiled smugly. "No. The Bible."

"Oh," Katie said, chastened. She smiled. "I knew that. I was just testing you."

Christina threw her small white airline pillow at her. "You did not!"

Katie went back to her seat and worked on her story. Christina opened a pack of Medicine cards. "This is a Native American form of foretelling destiny," she explained. "I'm trying to teach myself. It's like the tarot, only it deals with nature. Think of a question you want to ask and I'll do a reading after I have a chance to figure this out."

"Okay," Molly agreed, fishing in the bag for a chip.

What would she ask? She had so many questions. Would she make it to space someday? Would she make it to Space Camp this summer? Would she conquer this eating disorder once and for all?

Even without Christina's reading, she had the idea that the answer to all these questions was yes.

She gazed out the window and blinked hard. There, sitting on a cloud was the pleasingly plump, purple-clad, jewel-encrusted Yurthinny Nuf enthusiastically forking into a huge gooey slab of chocolate cake. Was *she* an angel? Had she been with Molly all through her time in the hospital? Or was she just a figment of Molly's imagination?

After all, Molly was beginning to realize that angels came in many forms.

Molly held her bag of chips up to the window. *I'm eating. See?* She said silently to the glamorous creature on the cloud.

Yurthinny Nuf smiled and winked at her.

Molly was sure of it.

FOREVER ANGELS

by Suzanne Weyn

Everyone needs a special angel . . .

Katie's Angel
0-8167-3614-6

Ashley's Lost Angel
0-8167-3613-8

Christina's Dancing Angel
0-8167-3688-X

The Baby Angel
0-8167-3824-6

An Angel for Molly
0-8167-3915-3

The Blossom Angel
0-8167-3916-1

The Forgotten Angel
0-8167-3971-4

Available wherever you buy books.

Troll